"I hate you," Zoe choked.

"You duped me all the way! We were safe in our little house. You made it impossible for us to stay there. You, and my grandfather playing your power games. And if you don't let go of me right now, I'm going to start screaming my head off!"

Pulling in a deep breath she opened her mouth to carry out the threat. Anton's mouth landed on hers with enough power to plug the threatened scream back down her throat. Even he was shocked that he'd used such a method to stop her. Yet once it was done, the idea of drawing back again did not enter his head. With her lips already parted and trembling with her tears, he felt their tongues touch, and heat exploded between them like some unknown powerful force. She was still sobbing but she kissed him back with hungry urgency. Where it had all come from he didn't think even she understood....

All about the author...
Michelle Reid

Reading has been an important part of **MICHELLE REID's** life as far back as she can remember, and was encouraged by her mother, who made the twice-weekly bus trip to the nearest library to keep feeding this particular hunger in all five of her children. In fact, one of Michelle's most abiding memories from those days is coming home from school to find a newly borrowed selection of books stacked on the kitchen table just waiting to be delved into.

There has not been a day since that she hasn't had at least two books lying open somewhere in the house, ready to be picked up and continued whenever she has a quiet moment.

Her love of romance fiction has always been strong, though she feels she was quite late in discovering the riches Harlequin Books has to offer. It wasn't long after making this discovery that she made the daring decision to try her hand at writing a Harlequin Presents novel for herself, never expecting it to become such an important part of her life.

Books by Michelle Reid

Harlequin Presents®
3001—AFTER THEIR VOWS
2934—MIA AND THE POWERFUL GREEK
(The Balfour Brides)

Michelle Reid

THE KANELLIS SCANDAL

TORONTO NEW YORK LONDON
AMSTERDAM PARIS SYDNEY HAMBURG
STOCKHOLM ATHENS TOKYO MILAN MADRID
PRAGUE WARSAW BUDAPEST AUCKLAND

ISBN-13: 978-0-373-13019-1

THE KANELLIS SCANDAL

First North American Publication 2011

This edition published by arrangement with Harlequin Books S.A.

For questions and comments about the quality of this book please contact us at Customer_eCare@Harlequin.ca.

www.Harlequin.com

Printed in U.S.A.

THE KANELLIS SCANDAL

CHAPTER ONE

THE assortment of telephones currently buzzing like angry wasps on his desk earned a flaring glance of impatience from Anton Pallis as he threw himself out of his chair and paced away from them down the length of his office.

He came to a stop in front of the floor-to-ceiling wall of glass which gave him unrivalled views of London's famous City skyline. A deep frown darkened his smooth, golden brow. Since the shock news reporting the death of Theo Kanellis's long-lost son had hit the news this morning, the stock market had gone into meltdown, and now those ringing telephones were attempting to take him to the same place.

'I understand the implications, Spiro,' he incised into the only phone he had deigned to take notice of. 'Which does not mean I am going to join in with everyone else and panic.'

'I did not even know that Theo had a son,' Spiro Lascaris declared in stunned incredulity that he had not been privy to such an important and potentially dangerous piece of information. 'Like most people, I believed that you were his heir.'

'I am not and never have been Theo's heir,' Anton denied, angry now that he had not bothered to scotch such rumours years ago when they had first started doing the rounds. 'We are not even distantly related.'

'But you lived as his son for the last twenty-three years!'

Anton threw back his dark head in a typically Greek negative gesture, because he so disliked being compelled to disclose anything to do with his relationship with Theo Kanellis. 'Theo took charge of my upbringing and education and that is all that he did,' he stated.

'As well as protecting your personal wealth and ensuring that the Pallis Group held its place at the top of the investment tree until you were old enough to take control,' Spiro pointed out. 'You can't tell me he did all of that out of the goodness of his heart.'

Because he did not have a heart, Spiro refrained from adding. Theo Kanellis was better known for his ruthless demolishing of other men's empires, not nurturing them.

'Admit it, Anton, Theo has been grooming you to take his place since you were ten years old, and everyone knows it.'

Anger flared to life inside Anton at Spiro's disparaging tone. 'Keep to the point of issue here,' he retaliated coldly. 'It is your job to work to squash any damaging rumours about the state of my relationship with Theo, not dig around in the dirt for more.'

The moment he'd finished speaking he sensed a change in atmosphere flowing down the telephone connection. He'd just pulled rank on one of his most trusted employees. 'Of course,' the lawyer in Spiro Lascaris came back coolly. 'I will get onto it straight away.'

The conversation finished with a distinctly chilly edge. With a snap of exasperation at the whole situation, Anton turned to stride back to his desk so he could toss the phone down on it along with the rest. It began ringing again almost immediately which did not surprise him. Anyone who was anyone in global finance was falling over themselves to find out what the death of Leander Kanellis—Theo's long-lost son—was going to mean to Anton's own current power-grip on Kanellis Intracom.

That was the real alarm bell ringing out there—not Anton's past relationship with Theo but his present relationship. He had been more or less running things for Theo since the old man had been taken ill two years ago and had retreated to his private island to live—although information about the seriousness of his illness had not yet found its way out there.

A small glimpse of light flickering in the midst of a raging storm, Anton mused grimly. Kanellis stock would not take yet another serious hit if it ever got out that Theo had been too sick to keep his finger on the pulse of his own business empire—which was the reason why Anton had allowed the general assumption to run that Theo was grooming him in preparation for the day when he would succeed him.

On a soft curse, he snatched up one of the phones again and called Spiro back to ensure his confidentiality with the information he had just imparted to him. Sounding stiff with offence that Anton had felt the need to remind him of such a basic ethic, Spiro promised that he would *never* divulge confidential information to anyone.

Laying the phone aside again, Anton swung round to rest his hips against the edge of his desk and frowned thoughtfully down at his shoes. He felt like a juggler, he realised with a brief, dry twist of a grimace: one ball demanded he keep Theo's business interests spinning happily up there in the air alongside his own global group of companies, another ball demanded he defend his own integrity and pride. And now a third ball had been tossed up there in the middle of the others, a far more unpredictable ball that belonged to the late Leander Kanellis—a man Anton only had a vague memory of, who had escaped from his arranged marriage at the youthful age of eighteen and had never been seen or heard of again.

Until now, that was, when the poor guy had turned up dead. A sigh slid from him. It was not even the death of Theo's previously forgotten son that was causing the current storm raging out there. No, it was the discovery that Leander had left a family behind him.

Legitimate Kanellis heirs.

Stretching out a long-fingered hand, Anton gathered up the tabloid that had broken the story and looked down at the photograph some bright young spark of a junior reporter had unearthed from somewhere. It showed Leander Kanellis standing with his family on what looked like a fun day out. There was a lake, trees and sunshine shimmering in the background. An old-fashioned wicker picnic-basket rested on the bonnet of an old-model sports car. In front of the car Leander Kanellis stood, tall, dark and very good-looking, and with a startling likeness to how Theo had looked several long decades ago.

Leander was laughing into the camera. Happy, Anton saw. Proud of the two women he held clasped beneath each substantial shoulder. Both women were fair-skinned blondes. The older one, Leander's wife, was so serenely beautiful it was no wonder their marriage had remained strong throughout twenty-three years of relative hardship—relative to what they could have had if Theo had not…

Anton stopped that thought before it formed fully, aware that the tension suddenly crushing his stomach muscles belonged to a previously alien sensation—guilt. From the age of eight, he had received the best of everything Theo's vast wealth could offer him while these people had struggled to…

Again he cut the thought short, not ready yet to deal with what it was going to mean to him.

Happy; he dealt with that phenomenon instead, because in its own way it was significant. If there was one thing that Theo's son had enjoyed which Anton had not experienced much of, then it was the happiness he could see shining out from all three people in this photograph.

His focus moved to the other female Leander hugged into his side. Though the photograph must have been an old one, because she looked about sixteen here, Zoe Kanellis was already showing promise of turning into a beauty made in her mother's image: the same long, slender figure and bright golden hair, the same shining blue eyes and wide sensual smile.

Happy. The word hit him again, like an ugly blow this time. There was another photograph printed alongside the first one which showed the now twenty-two-year-old version of Leander's daughter leaving the hospital with the newest member of her family cradled protectively in her arms. Shock and grief had wiped out the happiness. She looked pale, thin and drawn.

Zoe Kanellis, leaving hospital with her new baby brother, the caption read. *The twenty-two-year-old was away at University in Manchester when her parents were involved in a fatal car accident last week. Leander Kanellis died at the scene from his injuries. His wife, Laura, survived only long enough to give birth to their son. The tragedy took place on the—*

The sound of a tentative knock on his door brought Anton's head up as Ruby, his PA, stepped into the room.

'What now?' he demanded curtly.

'I'm sorry to disturb you, Anton,' she apologised with a fleeting glance at the still-buzzing phones. 'Theo Kanellis is on my main line and he's demanding to speak to you.'

A choice curse rattled around the tight casing of his ribs as he put the newspaper down then straightened up from the desk. He stood for a second, actually seriously considering turning chicken and refusing to take Theo's call.

But, no, he could not do that—as Ruby had known he couldn't, which was why she had interrupted him.

'OK. Put him through.' Anton strode around his desk and lowered himself back down into his chair, picked up the phone and waited for Ruby to connect the call.

He knew what was coming. Hell, he knew what was coming.

'*Kalispera*, Theo,' he greeted smoothly.

'I want the boy, Anton.' Theo Kanellis's famously hard and irascible voice sounded in his ear. 'Get me my grandson!'

'I didn't know you were a Kanellis,' Susie said, eyeing with an expression of awe the famous business logo belonging to Kanellis Intracom which headed the letter Zoe had just discarded on the kitchen table with a contemptuous flick of her hand.

'Dad dropped the "Kan" when he came to England to live.' *Because he was scared of being hunted down and dragged back to Greece by his bully of a father and forced into doing his duty,* she tagged on bitterly, though she gave a different reason to Susie. 'He thought Ellis was an easier name to use here in the UK.'

Susie's eyes were still round as saucers. 'But you've always known you are a Kanellis?'

Zoe nodded. 'It's on my birth certificate.'

And now it was on Toby's birth certificate, she added silently, her eyes glossing over when she recalled where else she had been forced to use the Kanellis name recently.

'I hate it,' she choked, fighting back the ever-threatening

burn of tears when she saw an image of herself sitting there looking at that name on two death certificates the same day that Toby's birth had been registered.

'Never mind about the name.' Reaching across the table, Susie squeezed one of her hands. 'I shouldn't have mentioned it.'

Why not? It was currently splashed all over every type of media there was out there, because some junior reporter for the local rag had happened to notice the Kanellis name while he'd been writing up the story about her parents' accident. He had been curious enough to follow it up with a clever bit of sleuthing. Zoe wondered if the same reporter would soon be working for one of the major tabloids; he certainly deserved the promotion for uncovering such a huge scoop.

'It feels weird,' Susie said, sitting back in her chair to look around the homely kitchen which doubled as a sitting-room cum everything-room.

'What feels weird?' asked Zoe, blinking tears from her eyes.

'That you are the granddaughter of a genuine, filthy-rich, Greek tycoon, yet you live right next door to me in an ordinary little house smack-bang in the middle of Islington.'

'Well, don't start imagining this is a real-life fairy tale.' Getting up from the table, Zoe carried their coffee mugs to the sink. 'Cinderella I'm not, and I don't want to be. Theo Kanellis—' she refused to refer to him or even think of him as 'Grandfather—is nobody to me.'

'That's not what this letter says, Zoe,' Susie pointed out. 'It says that Theo Kanellis wants to get to know you.'

'Not me—Toby.'

Turning around, she folded her arms across the ache constantly in control of her body, unaware that she was highlighting just how much weight she had lost over the last few, awful weeks. Her hair, usually a bright and shining golden colour, hung dull and heavy from a scraped-back pony tail which emphasised the strain in charge of her face. Dark shadows circled her blue eyes and her once naturally-smiling mouth had developed a permanent down turn that only lifted when she held her brother Toby.

'The horrible man disowned his own son! He never once attempted to acknowledge my mother while she was alive—or me, for that matter. And the only reason he's showing some interest in us now is because he's been shamed into it by all the negative press coverage he's getting. And because he probably fancies moulding Toby into a better clone of himself than he made of my father.' She sucked in a deep breath that turned out to be a suppressed sob. 'He's a cold and heartless, miserable old despot and he is *not* getting his hands on Toby!'

'Wow.' Susie breathed after a second of stunned silence. 'That's one heavy chip you carry on your shoulders there.'

You bet that it's heavy, Zoe thought bitterly. With a bit of loving support from his thankless father, her father might not have spent the last twenty-three years tinkering with, coaxing and lovingly polishing the ancient sports-car he'd brought with him to England when he'd run away from a marriage made with the devil. It was only now, when she woke up sobbing in the night visualising the whole horrid accident, that it occurred to her that her father had needed to hang onto the stupid old car because it was his only link to home. With a more caring father of his own maybe—just maybe—her father would have been driving her mother to the hospital in something newer and more substantial. Then maybe—just maybe—the car would have protected them from the full force of the impact that had killed them both.

And she would still be in Manchester right now, studying

for her post-grad and Toby, sleeping upstairs in the little room his parents had so excitedly prepared for him, would not have been robbed of the most loving parents a little boy could have.

Wow, she thought, echoing Susie as she drew the burning flood to a stop.

'It says here that you're to expect a visit from his representative this morning at eleven-thirty.' Susie had returned to the letter again.

Theo Kanellis was sending a representative to deal with her because he couldn't be bothered to come and do the job for himself.

'That means he should be here any minute.'

Just another person in the long line of people Zoe had had walking in and out of her life over the last three horrible weeks: doctors, midwives, care workers, a hundred different departments from social services wanting to check if she was a fit carer for her baby brother, or if she qualified for any handouts. Each one of them had arrived sporting tediously long tick-box questionnaires that had intruded on her privacy but which she'd had to answer if she wanted to hang on to Toby. Yes, she had left her university studies to look after her brother. Yes, of course she was prepared to take employment if child-care facilities came with the job. No, she did not have a boyfriend she might be thinking of moving in with her. No, she was not promiscuous or irresponsible. Of course she wouldn't leave Toby alone in the house while she went off to enjoy a girly night out. The inquisitions had gone on and on, each one of them filled with such horribly intrusive questions her skin still prickled with pique.

And then there had been the funeral people, she remembered, quiet, calm and very professional as they had walked her gently through the decisions regarding the worst arrangements a grieving daughter could ever have to make. Those arrangements had taken place three days ago and her grandfather had sent no *representative* to watch his only son and daughter-in-law being lowered into the ground. Had that absence been due to an awareness of the media hype, or due to sheer indifference?

Zoe didn't know and right at this precise moment she did not care. He had not turned up. He'd stayed hidden away in his ivory tower while the press had crawled all over the funeral like feeding locusts.

Which brought her nicely to the final list of people she'd been forced to deal with these last three awful weeks—the cockroaches out there who'd crawled out of the woodwork the same day the sensational story had broken. The ones that had come banging on her door to offer her big money for exclusive rights to her story, and the ones that still camped outside her home just waiting for her to step out of the door so they could pounce. Were they out there because they cared about her and Toby's tragic loss? No. They were there because Theo Kanellis was a recluse who hid himself away on his private island somewhere in the middle of the Aegean, and protected his privacy so well that this story was like a juicy, ripe peach they couldn't resist gobbling up—even if the juice was messy and the centre held a nasty, crawling worm.

Even the worm had a juicy name: Anton Pallis. The tall, dark and gorgeous global sex-icon and seriously clever CEO of the heavyweight Pallis Group. Pallis wasn't so picky about getting his name in the papers, business or pleasure. She'd often seen him making a name for himself. What she hadn't known until this story had broken, was that he was the man who had reaped the rewards of her father's exile.

A buzz of anger fizzed inside her like a tightly wound

ball of living energy, generated almost exclusively by that name—Anton Pallis. Every so often, especially when she let herself dwell on the name, that ball of energy broke free from its restraints and totally overwhelmed her need to remain sunk inside her desperate grief. Was this the Greek side of her she had never previously known she had coming to the surface—this burning desire to feed an unforgiving hate?

The front doorbell gave a sharp double ring suddenly. The two women tensed then looked at each other.

Susie got to her feet. 'Could just be one of the press trying their luck again,' she suggested.

But somehow Zoe just knew it was Theo Kanellis's *representative.* The letter had stated he would be calling on her at eleven-thirty and it was exactly eleven thirty as far as she could tell from the old clock hanging on the wall opposite. Wealthy men with loads of power expected their instructions to be carried out to the second, she thought grimly as she straightened up to her full five feet six inches, pushed back her narrow shoulders and pulled in a breath.

So this was it, the moment she found out what Theo Kanellis really wanted. She didn't doubt for a second that he was about to place an utterly obscene price on Toby's vulnerable little head.

'Do you want me to stay?'

Heavily pregnant with her second baby, Susie sounded genuine in her offer, but Zoe could read the uncertainty in her face. For all she'd been a wonderful neighbour and friend over the last devastating weeks—sneaking in the back way so no one could catch her, refusing to speak to the press each time she left her own house to do ordinary things like shopping or collecting her little girl from her playgroup up the street—Zoe knew Susie would prefer to back out of this particular scene.

'It's almost time for you to go and collect Lucy,' she reminded Susie, knowing that this was something she needed to face all by herself.

'If you're sure? I'll just slip out the back way, then.'

The doorbell rang again, jerking both women into movement. Susie made for the back door as Zoe went in the other direction. She heard the back door closing behind Susie as she came to stop at the solid wood door at the front of the house. Her throat felt dry suddenly and she swallowed. Her heart had acquired a couple of extra beats. Rubbing her palms nervously down the sides of her jeans, she took a minute to school her expression into something cold and unforthcoming then finally reached out to unlock the door.

In her mind she was expecting some short and stocky middle-aged Greek, with 'tough lawyer' stamped all over him. So when she drew open the door and saw exactly who it was standing there, surprise rendered her frozen by shock.

Tall, dark, immaculately presented, he looked like an exotic, dark prince clothed in an Italian suit. Handsome didn't even begin to describe his smooth, gold, angular features, or the pair of deep-set eyes the colour of midnight which held her own blue eyes trapped like powerful magnets. She had never looked into eyes like them. They made her feel slightly queasy because it felt as if they were trying to draw her in. When the noise suddenly started up as the media frenzy erupted, she still couldn't break free of them. He was so tall, he almost blocked out everything that was happening behind him—reporters shouting questions at them, TV camera-men and photographers locked in scuffles as they vied for position in their efforts to get the best shot.

He just continued to stand there as if it wasn't happening, protected by a semi-circle of space created by three big-set men wearing immaculate black suits who stood with their backs to him forming a tough-guy ring of protection around his personal space.

Finally managing to drag her gaze downwards a little, Zoe found herself staring at the uncompromisingly sensual shape to his unsmiling mouth. Inside she was a mixed-up mess of stirring emotions she couldn't even recognise. She was even mesmerised by his whole dynamic breath-stopping stance—the never-a-hair-out-of—place demeanour he was displaying, the relaxed set of his wide shoulders inside the dark jacket which didn't quite obscure the long lean rock-solid contours of his body beneath a crisp white shirt and sober dark tie. The sheer elegant quality of his whole manner screamed indomitable self-confidence at Zoe and drove the power of his personality home, a million stinging pinpricks attacking her unsuspecting flesh.

For the first time in three weeks, she became acutely aware of her own shabby appearance—the old pair of jeans she had dragged on this morning that had seen better days and the itchy knowledge that her hair was in need of a good wash. One of her hands clutched the edges of an old red cardigan together across the pounding pump going on behind her ribs. The cardigan was her mother's and she'd been wearing it all week, a big, fluffy, unsightly thing she hugged to her for comfort and because it kept giving her wafts of her mother's delicate scent.

He parted those beautifully moulded pair of lips and spoke to her. 'Good morning, Miss Kanellis,' he greeted in the most quietly modulated and beautiful voice. 'I believe you are expecting me.'

He sent Zoe's head reeling for a completely different reason: for the smooth, deep cultured tones of his Greek accent sounded so like her father's voice to her that it actually physically hurt.

Anton watched as Zoe closed her eyes and swayed in front of him. She looked as if she was going to faint. If he'd thought she'd looked stricken when she'd stood on the steps of the hospital in the photograph three weeks ago, it was nothing to how she looked right now—brittle. She looked painfully brittle, white-faced, pinched and frail enough for a puff of wind to blow her off her feet.

Biting back a soft curse, he acted on instinct and stretched out a hand with the intention of catching hold of her but she opened her eyes again, saw his hand coming towards her and shrank away from it as if it was an attacking snake.

Shock stunned him into stillness for a second. Something close to affront clawed down his front; it took grim grit and determination to stop his feelings from showing on his face. Aware of the media circus going on behind him, he tried to think fast. She did not need all of these witnesses watching her every move and expression. He did not want them to read her expression. What he needed was to get the two of them inside the house with the door shut before she stopped staring at him like that and started spitting insults at him—or, worse, slammed the door in his face.

'Shall we…?' he murmured very smoothly and took a step forward into the house.

As he was about to take the door from her grasp so he could close it, Zoe snatched her hand away from the risk of his touch. A fresh flare of affront struck at his pride but he kept on going, swinging the door shut behind him without allowing his expression to reveal anything—he hoped.

Silence clattered around them the moment the door closed. She was several feet away from him by now, hovering like a trapped bird, with her face still frighteningly pale and her eyes still fixed on his face.

She had the most startling pair of electric-blue eyes,

he noticed, and a trembling crushed-strawberry mouth. Something kicked into life low down in his gut but he ignored the sensation, annoyed with himself for feeling such a fierce sexual tug at a time like this.

'My apologies,' he said gravely, 'For entering your home without your invitation to do so. I thought it best that we conduct our business without all the witnesses looking on.'

She didn't speak. She just blinked at him, long—indecently long—golden-brown eyelashes moving in a slow movement; he had the weirdest feeling that she wasn't even seeing him. And she was clutching the most peculiar red garment across her breasts as if it was the only thing holding her upright.

'Let me try again,' he persisted, vaguely aware that they were standing in a hellishly narrow hallway with a set of steep stairs shooting up on his left. 'My name is—'

'I know who you are,' Zoe breathed out in a trembling whisper.

He was the man whose name had been bandied about in the media as much as her own name had been. He was the man Theo Kanellis had put in her father's place.

'You're Anton Pallis.'

Theo Kanellis's adopted son and heir.

CHAPTER TWO

A NEW kind of silence tumbled down between them. It crackled and spat with what Zoe Kanellis was not saying, though Anton saw her contempt for him beginning to write itself on her face.

He offered a wry smile. 'You have heard of me, then.'

The way she shot his smile a shrivelling glance killed it dead. 'I would need to be deaf and blind not to have heard of you, Mr Pallis,' she cut back, then just spun on her heels and walked off towards the rear of the house, leaving him to follow—or not. Her manner told him she was certainly not going to give him encouragement either way.

You are going to owe me big time for this one, Theo, Anton mused grimly as he took a moment to take in more of his surroundings. The house was tiny, a typical Victorian mid-terrace property with a steep, narrow staircase and two pine doors leading off the hall. It was all nicely decorated and a fawn-coloured carpet covered the floor. But, if he'd ever bothered to wonder how Leander Kanellis had lived since he'd walked away from one of Greece's wealthiest families, not in a million years would he have imagined he lived like this.

Zoe had disappeared through the farthest door; pulling in a breath, Anton followed in her wake. He found her standing in a surprisingly large kitchen which seemed to double up as a sitting room, a big, blue sofa and chair forming a comfortable seating-area. A television occupied one corner. A coffee table littered with tabloid newspapers stood between it and the sofa. The other half of the room was mainly taken up by a large wooden table dominating the floor space around which cheap, pine units were fixed to the walls.

He saw the baby paraphernalia stacked up on top of one of the units, the kind of things that were completely alien to him except in a purely abstract sense. A tiny cot-like thing stood near the sofa, though he could see no baby lying in it.

'He's asleep upstairs.'

She'd caught him looking. Turning around to face her, Anton opened his mouth to ask if the boy was doing OK, but she got in first.

'The media hype out there disturbs him when he's down here, especially when they start ringing the bell. So I put him to sleep upstairs at the back of the house where the noise doesn't carry so much.'

'You did not contact the police to have them moved away?' he asked, frowning.

She stared at him as if he'd just grown an extra head. 'We are not the royal family, Mr Pallis. The police say they can't do anything, and asking that lot to give us our privacy at this sad time doesn't work for us. Excuse me for a moment.'

Feeling like he'd just received a slap on the wrist for being so stupid, Anton watched as she turned and let herself out through the back door. For the strangest few seconds he thought she was going to do a runner and leave him standing here like a dumped fool. But as he watched her through the kitchen window he saw her walk down the length of what looked like a flower bedecked bower crushed into a tiny space and stop at a solid-wood back gate, then proceed to slide home two heavy bolts.

Maybe he'd deserved the slapped wrist, he allowed as it hit him that she was having to virtually barricade herself in here—though the evidence that the gate required bolting made him wonder who had sneaked out the back way before she had allowed him in the front. A man? A boyfriend? Had they been forced by the media activity out there to carry on their love affair by stealth?

For some reason he did not want to delve into too deeply, the idea of Zoe Kanellis lying in her lover's arms ten minutes before he'd arrived here did not sit well with him. He had plans for Zoe Kanellis that did not include the irritation of having to get rid of a lover.

Having secured the gate after Susie's recent departure, Zoe used her time outside to pull herself together. To have, of all people, Anton Pallis turn up on her doorstep had been shock enough, but to hear his voice sounding so like her father's had left her feeling weepy and faint. Could it not be enough for him that he walked in her father's shoes? Did he have to sound like him too?

She used up another few minutes by un-pegging the clothes she had hung to dry on the washing line this morning, building up her defences at the same time. She could not afford to show vulnerability in front of Anton Pallis. She knew why he was here. It was just a case of staying strong enough to stone-wall whatever offer he was about to put on the table—while ignoring his voice at the same time.

Oh Dad, she thought helplessly, pausing to close her eyes for a second while she just wished he was here with her. Her wonderful father with his quiet, gentle ways and his oh, so understated air of pride. He would have known how to deal with the likes of Anton Pallis, especially with her beautiful mother standing by his side.

But none of this would be happening at all if they had been here, Zoe reminded herself. No, it was just her on her own left to protect Toby from the grasping clutches of Theo Kanellis—via the man standing in her kitchen right now.

Stepping back inside, she found he was still standing where she had left him, in the process of sliding a mobile phone into his pocket. He dwarfed the room with the sheer power of his personality. Everything about him was larger than life and so expensively honed and neat. His charcoal suit draped his powerful figure with creaseless silkiness; his facial features were so perfectly balanced even his high-bridged nose didn't look out of place. Nor did the thick and glossy satin-black hair so perfectly cut to flatter the shape of his head nor the sheen to his closely shaven chiselled chin.

He glanced up and caught her staring at him, and Zoe felt those pin pricks attack her flesh again.

'I have arranged for you to have some security to keep the media away.'

'Oh good,' she said, looking away from him and tipping her armload of washing onto the table. 'Now Toby and I can go out surrounded by heavy bruisers instead of reporters. What a treat.'

Sensing a sharpening in his mood at her ungrateful tone, she began folding baby clothes.

'Would you like me to do more?' he enquired.

It was a serious question, Zoe recognised, cushioned with genuine concern. 'I don't recall asking you to do anything,' she responded. 'But then, hey—' she shrugged '—I did not ask for any of this. Would you like a coffee or something before you begin your pitch?'

Anton narrowed his eyes. What he had seen in her as brittle and frail had been a dangerous miscalculation, he realised. For whatever the physical ravages grief had wrought on Zoe Kanellis, she was sharp-tongued and tough. In one way he supposed he should have been ready for it—she was Theo's granddaughter, after all.

And she hated him; he'd seen that already. She probably hated Theo too. If she was as intelligent as her CV said she was, then she had also worked out exactly why he was here and was more than ready to take on the fight.

'Your grandfather—'

'Stop.' Dropping the pale-blue body suit she had been folding, Zoe spun on her heels to send him a cold look. 'Let's get one thing clear before we start this, Mr Pallis—the person you refer to as my grandfather is nobody to me. So you will please use his proper name—or, even better, don't mention him at all.'

'Well, that cuts the need for conversation between us down to nil before it even gets started,' he mocked.

Another shrug and she returned to folding the washing. Anton studied her while he contemplated the different ways he could tackle this. He had not come here expecting it to be easy, but nor had he come here expecting to find Zoe Kanellis so ravaged by grief or filled with so much bitterness for a man she had never been given the chance to meet.

'I expected him to send a lawyer.'

'I am a lawyer,' Anton told her, surprised that she'd given him something with which to set the ball rolling. 'I trained as one at least, though I rarely have the opportunity to use the skill these days.'

'Too busy being the hot-shot tycoon?'

Relaxing slightly, he smiled. 'Life in the fast lane,' he conceded, 'I am rarely in one place long enough to utilise the concentration required by the law. I believe your thing is astrophysics—much more impressive.'

'Was,' she replied. 'And before you start explaining to me how easy you can make it for me to go back to my studies, I am not willing to hand over my brother to anyone, even for a pot of gold,' she added flatly.

'I don't believe I was intending to offer a pot of gold,' Anton countered. 'Or to explain to you what you clearly already know.'

'Which is what?'

'That you can probably get a government grant to help you with child care while you continue your studies.'

Picking up the stack of folding washing, she moved across the kitchen to put the things down on top of another pile of washing. 'You've been doing your homework.'

'It's the lawyer in me,' he answered. 'I also know that you cannot remain living here to bring up your brother and continue your studies, because the mortgage on this house was not protected by life insurance so it still must be paid.'

Zoe turned to look at him again. It amazed her how he could dare to stand there looking so relaxed while discussing her life as if it was his business!

'Did your boss tell you to mention that?'

'My boss?' he arched a sleek black eyebrow.

'Theo Kanellis. The guy who gave you your great start in life, then turned you into his messenger boy.'

At last she had the satisfaction of seeing a stab of anger flare his nostrils. 'Your *grandfather* is old and sick and unable to travel far.'

He'd used the 'grandfather' label deliberately, Zoe noted. 'Though not too old and sick to throw his weight around,' she countered.

'You are not very sympathetic to his age and his health, are you?' he drawled in return.

'No, not at all,' she confirmed. 'In fact you can take it as a given that I couldn't care less if he sent you here to tell me had was about to drop dead.'

She turned away to click the switch on the kettle, so she missed the way Anton used the moment to narrow his eyes in grim contemplation of his foe.

'However, in any other circumstance he wasn't likely to bother with *any* message for me, was he?' she went on as she turned back again in time to watch him lower glossy black eyelashes over his eyes. 'It's only that he wants Toby so he can groom him into a chip off the old block more worthy of the Kanellis name than my father was that he's bothered to send you here at all.'

As he parted his lips to respond to all of that, Zoe watched him change his mind and clip those beautiful lips together again in a way that held her ever so slightly transfixed. How old was he? she wondered. Late twenties, early thirties? Not much more than that.

'You are very bitter,' he observed quietly.

'Look around you,' Zoe invited. 'Does this look like the home of a Greek billionaire's family?'

He did it. He actually dared to stand there in her cluttered kitchen and look around at the pine cupboards, cheap lino and the two mugs sitting on the draining board waiting to be washed. The pure silk of his suit slithered expensively against his long body as he moved.

Then she caught the brief twist his horribly sensual mouth gave and her offended dignity suddenly caught light. 'If I wipe down a chair would you like to sit down?'

He swung back on her so sharply Zoe almost jumped, then wished she could take the snipe back again when she saw the sudden, hard glint in his eyes. 'Now, that was uncalled for,' he rebuked.

'Well, don't make remarks about my feelings for a man

I have never met or even heard a peep out of in my twenty-two years,' she threw back. 'And don't,' she added warningly, 'Even attempt to defend him by telling tales about how badly my father let him down or I will be showing you the door, Mr Pallis—or killing the messenger.'

She couldn't stop the last bit—it just came out. A tight silence dropped between them. Zoe could not take her eyes off the sudden stillness in control of his face. Her heart had picked up extra beats again and those prickles were making themselves felt as she waited for him to retaliate. When he took a step towards her, she raised her chin up in defiance even as her eyes revealed that she knew that this time she had gone too far with her snipes.

'Don't touch me,' she jerked out as he raised a hand then made her stiffen and drag in a breath as he closed his fingers around her wrist. It was only when he brought up his other hand to carefully prise the knife she hadn't been aware that she was holding from her fingers that she realised what he was doing.

Maintaining his grip on her wrist, he leant past her to drop the knife back on the counter top. The move brought him close, too close, overwhelming her suddenly with his superior height and the amount of leashed power lurking beneath the suit. Her next breath feathered its way across her throat when she picked up his clean, masculine scent.

'OK, Miss Kanellis,' he murmured. 'Let us take it as a given that we don't like each other. However, heed my advice when I suggest that you stick to using words to try piercing me with; knives tend to draw blood.'

Her cheeks heated up. 'I was not intending to—'

'I meant *your* blood, Zoe,' he whispered soberly. He held onto her eyes for a few mind-stinging seconds then let go of her wrist and took a step back.

He really confused her when he relaxed his wide

shoulders and offered her a smile—or half of one. 'I could do with that cup of coffee you offered to make me.'

Flustered by the whole macho demonstration, Zoe stared as he pulled out a chair at the table then lowered himself gracefully into it. Even that had been done as a stab at her insolent manner.

Crushing her lips together, she turned her attention to the kettle and wished the uncomfortable flush would cool from her cheeks. Half of it was there because she was so angry with herself for losing the high ground with her unwitting gesture with the knife; she hadn't even noticed that she'd picked it up from the breadboard.

Talk about mind transference, she mocked as she poured boiling water onto instant-coffee granules.

'Do you want milk and sugar?' she asked him.

'No thank you, to both.'

'A biscuit then?' Never let it be said that her mother had not taught her good manners; she mocked herself yet again.

There was another of those hesitations behind her before he answered, 'Yes, why not?'

His manners were coming back out for an airing, Zoe recognised as she reached up to open a cupboard and took out a packet of digestives. She knew he didn't really want the darn biscuit—but two 'no thank you's would have made him appear churlish so he'd taken the gracious route.

She placed the two coffees and a plate of biscuits down on the table then sat down on a chair opposite his. Outside the sun was shining in through the kitchen window, casting a sunbeam across the table top. As he picked up his coffee, Zoe watched the sunbeam touch the honey-brown skin of his long fingers as they curled around the mug. Her insides were churning and she knew why. Normally she avoided conflict, would run away from it if she could. Yet here she was intentionally goading Anton Pallis into a row. And really she knew she wasn't being fair because none of this was his fault.

'Scapegoat,' he said, bringing her chin shooting upwards. He sent her a wry kind of look. 'You need to grind your axe on someone and I happen to be handy. But your fight is not with me, you know. It's with Theo.'

He really believed that? 'Tell me,' she countered. 'How does it feel to walk in my father's shoes?'

Right there he had it, Anton noted without allowing himself to react: the reason why she'd shrunk away from him at the front door earlier. Why she hated him so much. She saw his relationship with her grandfather as the sole reason her father had been left out in the cold.

A baby's demanding cries suddenly impinged on the tension sizzling between them across the table. Perhaps it was good thing, he mused as he watched her rise to her feet. She'd gone pale again, he noticed, was maybe even a little ashamed of herself. Without saying a single word, she walked out of the room.

Left alone, he sat staring into his coffee, not frowning, not doing anything, because in truth he knew that for all its intended insult the stab about her 'father's shoes' held a nucleus of truth. How was he to know what might have happened between Theo and his son if he had not been there to fill the gap left by Leander's dramatic parting?

In the silence of the untidy kitchen, he sent another curse out to Theo for being so stubborn and making this situation what it now was.

Toby's room was almost as tiny as the full-sized cot standing in it. But it was as pretty as a picture, all white and pale blue, with splashes of fire-engine red. Zoe had tried to convince her parents to give the baby her larger bedroom because she was away at uni most of the time, but they'd refused, insisting that the room was *her* room—and anyway this room was the perfect size for a small baby.

A baby they'd yearned twenty years for. Just when they had believed their chances had passed them by, this little angel had been conceived. And Zoe loved him. She loved him so much her heart swelled as she reached into the cot and picked her brother up.

He was wet and he was grizzly but he recognised her voice and opened his eyes when she said softly, 'No one is taking you away from me, my darling.'

Taking time to change him out of his wet things, she made him comfortable then carried him downstairs. The noise outside seemed to be getting worse and she frowned as she walked down the hallway, wondering what could have excited them all to such a degree.

The reason for the increased noise stood in front of the kitchen window with his back to the room. It must have got round that Anton Pallis was here. All it would take next would be for a helicopter to land in the street and for Theo Kanellis to step out, and the press would feel like all their wildest dreams had come true.

Greek billionaires converge on tiny terrace in Islington! Zoe wrote the headline as she went to collect Toby's bottle from the fridge.

This billionaire was talking into his mobile phone again. Something really alien curled up her tummy muscles as she looked at him. It wasn't attraction, exactly, she told herself, though she would be lying if she did not acknowledge he was very good to look at—all height and width and long, lean elegance encapsulated in your typical million-dollar suit.

Dragging her eyes away from him, she listened to him talking in Greek as she busied herself. He was angry about something and when he heard her moving about and glanced around there was an impatient frown on his face. Finishing the telephone conversation abruptly, he rested back against the sink unit, accessed a number in his directory then the phone was back at his ear again.

Zoe stopped listening. Walking round to the sofa, she kicked off her slip-ons and curled herself cross-legged into the corner then bent her head to concentrate on coaxing Toby to accept the bottle teat.

She'd only met the man half an hour ago yet already this scene felt so unnaturally *natural*, she mused as she stroked Toby's baby-soft cheek: her sitting here feeding a baby, while he leant against the kitchen sink at the other end of the room, coolly relaying a series of instructions in what sounded remarkably like Russian to her.

A vision of domestic bliss, she mocked it, catching hold of Toby's waving starfish hand and lowering her head to brush it with a kiss.

He finished his call, and all went quiet in the kitchen. She could hear the wall-clock ticking and soft hum of the fridge. There was tension in the air too, mostly due to the last words she had thrown at him before she'd gone to get Toby, she supposed. She should not have said it, and remorse had been eating away at her ever since. She had no right whatsoever to blame this man for being Theo Kanellis's substitute son. She might not be sure just how old Anton Pallis was, but it didn't take many brain cells to work out that he could only have been a child when he'd been put in her father's place. And her father had always claimed that he'd walked away from that life of his own volition and had never felt the slightest desire to go back to it again.

For a man who had never experienced discomfort in any environment, Anton discovered he was feeling it here in the home of Leander Kanellis. Zoe's remark about him walking in the other man's shoes was still cutting deep, he acknowledged.

'You and your brother could have so much more than this,' he heard himself utter as one thought led him to another place—the natural negotiator in him, Anton recognised.

Zoe looked up at him over the back of the sofa and caught him indulging in a rueful grimace.

'And the price?' she asked out of sheer curiosity.

Attempting to ease some of the tension out of his shoulders without her noticing, Anton strode forward, skirting around the table to come to a halt at the armchair which matched the blue sofa.

'May I…?' he requested politely.

She shrugged a narrow shoulder then nodded, and he lowered himself into the chair. It was surprisingly comfortable, he discovered, though he did not relax into it but sat forward to place his forearms on his thighs.

He seemed about to open negotiations by extolling Theo's virtues; she spoke first. 'I'm sorry for what I said to you earlier. It was totally unfair.'

'No, don't do that.' Anton frowned and shook his head. 'Don't apologise to me for anything you say. You have the absolute right to speak what you believe is the truth. And you know why I've come here.'

'Perhaps you'd better put it in words so there will be no misunderstandings, then.'

It was not a climb down from hostilities which made her offer the invite, and Anton did not take it as one. But at least she was opening a line of discussion he was more comfortable with—business. The business side of their meeting was about to begin.

'I am here to negotiate terms on which you will agree to hand Theo his grandson. Theo does not mind if you come with the deal, but if you want to return to your studies he's offering to support you all the way.'

'Well, thank him for me, but tell him no thank you,' Zoe returned politely. 'Toby is my brother and we stick together—here in England.'

'And if Theo decides to push for custody of his grandson?'

She didn't even flinch at the suggestion. 'I am Toby's legal guardian,' she stated. 'And I don't think Theo Kanellis will risk the bad press by attempting to contest me on that.'

His eyes were intent on her. 'Are you sure about that?'

'Absolutely.' She nodded.

So did Anton, and pressed his lips together and dropped the subject. 'Theo is not a bad man.' He tried a different tack. 'He is tough and he is stubborn, and sometimes he is infuriatingly impossible to deal with, but he is not dishonest or corrupt or cruel to children.'

'But he couldn't be bothered to send a representative to his own son's funeral.'

'Admit it,' Anton fired back. 'You would have despised him for it if he had done.'

'No-win situation then,' she acknowledged, and brought his attention to the scrap of a thing she held in her arms when she deprived the boy of his bottle and he let out a protesting squeak.

Lifting him up onto her shoulder, she began gently patting his tiny back. The half-finished bottle of formula rested in the crook of her lap. She looked incredibly young and vulnerable suddenly—they both did—Anton observed and felt like the devil's messenger come to steal a baby—cold, ruthless and sure of himself.

'Your grandfather has been very ill and is unable to travel far.'

For a second he thought he detected a flicker of softening in her eyes until she said, 'Ill for twenty-three years, at a guess.'

He did not pretend to misunderstand her. 'Your father—'

'Don't!' Suddenly, warning sparks were flying from her electric-blue eyes. 'Don't even attempt to heap the blame on my father because I won't listen! He is not here to defend himself any more which makes that line of negotiation low and cheap.'

'My apologies,' Anton said instantly.

'Not accepted,' Zoe threw back, still fizzing inside with anger on behalf of her father. The baby let out a whining squeak. Settling the small boy into the crook of her arm again, she retrieved his bottle and offered it to the cherub-like mouth.

Anton watched, momentarily fascinated. He had no experience with babies, or children of any age for that matter, but the one thing he noticed about this baby was that, in every way he could see from here, he was Greek. The head of black hair, the light olive tone to his skin, even the demand for attention, said 'typical Greek male' to him.

'That boy you are holding deserves the best kind of life you can offer him, Zoe.' Tough though it was, Anton knew from experience that it was the truth. 'To deprive him of the best because you refuse to forgive your grandfather his sins is unforgivably selfish and wrong.'

'Why don't you just *shut up* and go away?' She launched at him in shocking full volume, making his soot-black eyelashes flicker in surprise and Toby jerk in her arms.

CHAPTER THREE

'I HATE you,' she could not resist whispering before she pulled in a deep tear-thickened breath in an effort to calm herself for the baby's sake.

'Because you know I am right,' Anton persisted. 'You know you cannot even afford to maintain this roof over your two heads, which will mean you moving into cheaper accommodation. It is a slippery road to destitution and misery, Zoe. A road you don't have to take.'

His mobile phone started ringing. With soft curse Anton rose to his feet, retrieving the phone from his pocket before striding off back down the kitchen to take the call. It was Kostas, his head of security, calling to warn him that trouble was brewing outside the house.

'The neighbours are out in force, and they are not happy,' Kostas told him. 'Their lives have been turned upside down by what's going on here. They want it to stop.'

Another phone started ringing. Anton turned to watch as Zoe uncurled from the sofa and went to answer it. He watched her face go pale as she listened to whoever it was doing all the talking, and witnessed the slump of her narrow shoulders as if someone had dumped a heavy weight on them.

'OK, Susie,' she mumbled. 'Yes. Thanks for warning me.'

'It's been coming for days, Zoe,' Susie told her. 'We

can't even park on our own street. Our doorbells are constantly ringing. They accost us if we dare to step outside. Lucy started crying when we came home this lunchtime because we were jostled as we tried to get into our own house.'

Toby sighed against her shoulder. Zoe felt the tremors of a helpless weariness take control of her legs. Eyes stinging, heart stinging, she tried to think of something reassuring to say but she just didn't have anything. And in the end she was actually glad when the phone was removed from her trembling fingers by a long-fingered hand.

'Go and sit down,' Anton Pallis instructed quietly.

She didn't even argue. It seemed pointless to try when she was barely managing to stand on her own two feet. Coiling back down on the sofa, she hugged Toby to her shoulder and listened to the deep voice speaking quietly behind her. He sounded like her father again. He was using the same even, mellow tones of a natural mediator.

The tears began to flow. This time she didn't bother to try and stop them. She'd never felt so miserable or so alone in her entire life. She missed them. She missed her father coming home from working at the local garage and stripping off his grease-stained mechanic's boiler-suit. No matter how tired he was, his handsome face had always broken into that wonderful, charismatic grin. She missed her mother, her soft, gentle mother—plump because she loved baking—walking down the kitchen and straight into his waiting arms. She missed the warmth, the homeliness and the laughter, the way they'd all squeeze onto the sofa to watch the current reality-TV show and argue constantly over who was the best contestant.

And she missed the love, the all-over, all-encompassing shelter of love they had surrounded themselves with here in this modest, always slightly untidy little house.

A love Toby was never going to know now.

The sofa sank as Anton came to sit down beside her. He passed an arm around her shoulders and drew her against his side like a coiled foetus. Toby was fast asleep. He was oblivious to everything.

'Listen to me, Zoe,' Anton urged her deeply. 'You must know you cannot continue to stay here. The situation out there is impossible for everyone concerned.'

'Make them go away, then,' she sobbed into his shoulder.

'I wish I could but I don't have that kind of power.'

'It's only got worse because you came here.'

'Then let me offer a way to make amends. I have a house with big secure gates and a high fence all around it. I can have you transported out of here and on your way there within the hour if you will agree. No strings attached,' he added when she pulled away from him, keeping her head down to hide her tear-blotched face. 'Think of it as a bolthole away from all of this. Somewhere to stay while you give yourself a chance to catch your breath and recover, build your strength up before we start negotiations again.'

Anton could see that she was listening, fighting back the tears while keeping her head tucked down over the boy's sleeping head.

'Think about it,' he urged, piling on the pressure while producing a neatly folded handkerchief from his pocket and handing it to her. She took it from him, which felt like a mild triumph. 'This has nothing to do with Theo. This is just me offering you what I believe you need right now—a sanctuary, if you like, set in pleasant surroundings. I will not be living there. I have business to attend to overseas for the next few weeks anyway, so you will have the place all to yourself.'

Anton knew he was not telling the absolute truth here. He knew that his killer instincts had kicked in and taken control the moment Zoe Kanellis had revealed her weakened state.

Zoe was trying to talk herself out of Anton's offer of a bolthole. She hated it that she had burst into tears in front of him too. He was a shark by nature and he knew when to circle his prey. She wasn't fooled by his 'no strings attached' offer. She knew the pulse of concern he was giving off was probably false and that what he was really doing was inching control of the situation over to himself.

But she also knew he was right about it being impossible for her to stay here while the press were still so interested in their story. Just thinking of little Lucy crying because she had been frightened by those awful people out there made her want to start weeping all over again.

'I want you to promise that you won't try to pressure me.' She sniffed into the handkerchief.

'You have my word.'

'And you won't tell my grandfather where I am.'

Did she know she'd just used the forbidden word 'grandfather'? 'That is a tough one, but I will try my best to keep him out of the loop.'

'And when I'm ready to come back home you won't try to stop me.'

'Scouts' honour,' Anton said.

It startled her into glancing up at him through her tear sparkling eyelashes. Anton responded to the glimpse of electric-blue suspicion by raising a black eyebrow and she released a tear-thickened laugh. He liked Zoe Kanellis, he realised. He liked her courage in the face of all this adversity and her— Well, he liked her in other ways that were totally inappropriate, given the situation.

Still, he could not resist daring another gesture by reaching up to brush a damp strand of hair from her cheek. She did not flinch away. In fact she didn't do anything. It was really quite weird, he decided, how they'd ended up sitting here staring at each other without either seeming to want to look away.

He did it; he blinked to break the connection then climbed gracefully back to his feet. 'Tell me what needs to be done here.'

Brisk and businesslike again, Zoe noted, as he glanced at his watch then dipped his hand in his pocket to collect his mobile phone. He looked energised, dynamic, excitingly gorgeous…

Standing up just as abruptly as he had done, she went to settle Toby into his cot, feeling awkward suddenly and unwilling to look at him again. 'I need to pack some things for myself and Toby, and I need to take a quick shower and change my clothes…' she rattled off quickly in an effort to cover up an attack of confusion. 'Does your house have baby facilities?'

'It will have by the time we reach it,' said the man used to organising anything. 'Go and do what you need to do. You can leave the boy where he is,' he added when she went to pick Toby up again. 'I'll watch over him.'

Zoe was about to demand if he knew how to look after a baby, but he'd already turned away and was talking on his phone. With a shrug, Zoe left him to it. There was a part of her—a lurking part—questioning if she knew what she was doing, placing herself and Toby in the hands of the enemy. But for some reason she did not want to look too deeply into the question. And it did not stop her from packing a couple of bags then slipping into the bathroom to take her shower.

By the time she came back downstairs again, Anton had been joined in the kitchen by a thick-set man wearing a black suit. They were talking in low voices but when they heard her step into the room both men stopped abruptly and looked at her. Zoe stilled, aware that she'd interrupted something important. Her gaze went from the newcomer's tough, impassive features to Anton's even harder-to-read face. Even his eyes had taken on a shadowy lustre which made her think of dark veils.

Those eyes scanned her then disappeared completely behind his thick black eyelashes for a second before he brought them back to her face. She thought she saw a muscle twitch at the corner of his mouth but could not be absolutely sure of it because the mouth then stretched out a brief smile.

'This is Kostas Demitris, my head of security,' he told her.

Drifting her blue gaze back to the other man she nodded her head in acknowledgment and he did the same back to her.

'Kostas will make sure his men see that your home is secure once we have left it,' Anton continued, bringing her gaze back to him. 'Anything you think you might need from here that we cannot take with us now, tell Kostas and he will see that it follows us. It also would be wise if you gather together any personal documents you have around the place, so we can take them with us too—for safe keeping.'

She parted her lips with the intention of questioning that particular command—and it had been a command, even if he'd made it sound like advice—but Anton got in first with, 'We can secure the house to the best of our ability but once we have left here we cannot predict the determination of certain—low life—if they decide to take a look around in here in search of a new scoop.'

Not liking the image that he'd just planted in her head, of some sleazy person deciding to ransack her home while she was away from it, once again Zoe parted her lips to say so.

'It is a precaution, nothing more,' he inserted again. 'Kostas likes to be thorough in his forward planning.'

Shifting her eyes back to the other man, he offered a confirming nod. 'Anton is used to this level of precaution, Miss Kanellis. It is the down side of living a high-profile life.'

Zoe took in a breath, ready to protest that her life wasn't high profile, then stopped herself. She could not argue that it was certainly high profile right now.

Both men were standing there waiting for her agreement. That questioning voice in her head asked her again why she was allowing them to take control like this. Then she thought of Lucy next door, scared and upset by those people out there; too-close-to the-surface tears formed together with an aching lump in her throat. With a mute nod, she gave them what they wanted, then walked over to Toby's cot and bent over it, glad that her freshly washed and dried hair slithered forward to hide the bleak expression on her face.

The scent of freshly sliced apples filtered up along the sunbeam glistening in the silky fall of her shining hair and entered Anton's nostrils. He had a battle on his hands not to inhale deeply. In truth he was struggling to keep a lot of things together, not least his libido, which had been in a state of stirring defiance since she'd walked back into the room. For the pale and thin, grief-stricken creature who had walked out of here half an hour ago showed little resemblance to the one he was looking at now.

This one was quite ravishingly beautiful, a breathtaking upgrade of the younger version he'd seen in the newspaper the day all of this had begun. Gone was the appalling baggy red cardigan, the scraped-back dull hair and the faded jeans. This version wore a dramatically plain shift dress in the most amazingly classy dove-grey jersey fabric which skimmed the fragile curves of her slender figure and finished halfway down the length of her long, slender thighs. OK, so the dress was a size too big right now because she had lost weight, but the promise of what still hid beneath it tantalised his imagination—as did the rest of her legs covered in stretchy black leggings and the delicacy of her slender white ankles elevated by her black platform shoes.

'I hope you know what you're doing,' Kostas growled at him in softly spoken Greek.

The sharp-sensed devil had picked up on what was happening to him, Anton realised. 'Just concentrate on your job,' he flipped back.

'She is—'

'This is probably a good moment to tell you that I am bilingual,' Zoe informed them both in beautifully fluid Greek as she straightened up from her brother's cot. She looked at them, vivid blue eyes like icy darts now. 'And I hope you do know what you are doing, Mr Pallis, because if you think you are softening me up to be a pushover, you could not be more mistaken if you tried.'

She did not miss the dark hue which coloured the face of Kostas Demitris as she said that, even though her gaze was focused on his employer, who showed no such embarrassment at being caught out discussing her in a language they'd believed she could not understand.

Anton Pallis merely relaxed his stance, leaning back against the kitchen sink again and slid his hands into trouser pockets. The action pushed back the edges of his jacket to display the long solidity of his muscular torso trapped inside the clean, crisp whiteness of his shirt and the delineating line of his slender silk tie. Something suspiciously close to sensual heat flared low in Zoe's belly as she grazed her eyes lower over his narrow hips then the long length of his legs to the shiny tops of his handmade leather shoes.

'So you don't hate everything Greek, then?' he murmured, bringing her gaze skittering all the way back up him again to become trapped by the spark of amusement she could see in his impossibly dark eyes.

She looked away again, but felt slightly breathless. 'I would have to hate my own father to do that.'

'And part of yourself, since you are half Greek. Get to it, Kostas,' he tagged on without changing the soft intonation in his voice.

Kostas Demitris muttered something beneath his breath as he jerked into movement. Feeling as if she was about to be left alone with a dangerous animal, Zoe turned chicken and decided to escape. 'Can I show you what I need bringing from upstairs?' she asked Kostas. 'And I will need to give you the box containing my personal papers.'

With that she walked back into the hallway, leaving Anton staring at his shoes, ruefully smiling to himself.

All hint of humour had left him as they assembled in the narrow hallway half an hour later. Kostas had control of the door; Anton stood against the wall, his demeanour silent and grim as he studied the downturned profile of Zoe Kanellis. What light application of make-up she had applied was useless as a cover up because the strain was back on her face—the ravaged hollows, the barely steady set of her lips. She had pulled on a black jacket and she was trying to fasten the buttons with fingers that shook. On the floor in front of her the baby slept on, oblivious to the silent tension pulsing all around him, Anton saw, looking at the contraption the child slept in which he'd been told doubled as a car safety-seat.

He wanted to touch her in reassurance. It played on his

senses like an itch he could not scratch. The pulling-on of the jacket had somehow placed a defensive space around her that he recognised instinctively would earn him another shrinking rejection, like the one he had suffered when he'd first arrived here, if he tried to cross it.

She did not want to do this, which was another reason why he was holding himself back from making any risky moves. She'd had time to think about what she'd agreed to and he held a suspicion that the only thing stopping her from changing her mind was the tempting prospect of the sanctuary he had promised her, with the all-important no strings attached.

Kostas was talking quietly into his mobile; he turned to send Anton a look. With a nod of his head he acknowledged it, aware that his conscience was not happy right now. He was a liar and he knew it. And the only reason why he was determined to let this continue was his belief that what he was doing was for hers and the boy's own good.

'My car is parked right outside the door.' He broke through the tension with his voice carefully level. 'My people will attempt to maintain a corridor for us to reach it. However, I am afraid we can do nothing about the way the media will react once they see us. It will be noisy and intimidating. The trick is to fix your attention on the open car door and walk straight into it.'

Zoe pressed her pale lips together and nodded that she understood.

'Try to keep in your mind that once *we* have left here *they* will leave, and your neighbours will retrieve their peace and quiet.'

Staring down at Toby sleeping snugly in his car seat, she nodded again.

'Will you allow me to take care of your brother?'

This time she looked up. Those amazing eyes were

burning with so many conflicting things, from uncertainty in what she was doing to straight-out anxiety and fear, that Anton broke his own constraints, reached out and rested his fingers beneath her chin. Her skin felt like the finest silk.

'Trust me.' He uttered his biggest lie yet, then watched her lips tremble as they parted.

'I do,' she told him.

It was no reassurance. In fact his own expression turned so tough even he felt its harshness as he bent to grasp the handle of the child's seat. As he straightened up again he looked at Kostas, who said something into his mobile then turned to open the door.

Zoe's heart was throbbing in her mouth even before the din hit her. The afternoon sunlight spilled over the threshold just before it was blocked out by Kostas's bulky shape. Anton placed an arm around her shoulders. She didn't protest when he drew her close into his side. They walked through the door in a huddle of dipped heads and baby seat. She did as she had been told to do and focused on the limousine standing there with a man at the ready to throw open the rear door.

There were flashes, shouts, the vague impression of a swirling crowd-surge. 'What does it feel like to be Theo Kanellis's granddaughter, Zoe? Hey, Anton, how does it feel to lose a fortune? Is it true Theo Kanellis wants the boy?'

His handsome face locked in austere lines, lips pinned together, Anton kept them walking. His own body blocked Zoe's transfer into the car. The baby seat followed, grabbed and hugged to Zoe's lap as he dipped his long body and followed her inside. One of his men closed the door. Her eyes were wide and stark with alarm. She almost jumped out of her skin when people started banging on the glass beside her, making her swing around wildly to find camera flashes blinding her eyes.

They started moving. Peeling her eyes forward, she saw the shadowy bulk of a uniformed driver separated from them by a partition of glass.

'Oh my God,' she choked as the sound of sirens suddenly wound into life. Blue lights started flashing in front and behind them. She twisted one way then the other. 'We have a police escort?' she gasped.

'It was the only way we could have forged a passage out of here,' her companion explained.

Clutching Toby's seat to her, she turned her wide eyes onto him. 'You're *that* important?'

'*We* are that important,' he corrected, almost nailing Zoe to her seat with the salient point.

Life as she knew it had just taken a hike, she registered fully for the very first time. It was never going to be the same again. She'd spent three weeks living in fairyland, blithely telling herself that if she just sat it out everyone would eventually go away and leave her and Toby alone.

Twisting in her seat, she glance backwards. 'The press are going to follow us,' she whispered, staring beyond the rear police-car to where she could see people making frantic dives towards their own transport.

'Though not, I hope, once we are in the air.'

That grabbed her attention away from the chasing pack, Anton noted, as she focused those incredible eyes back on him. 'The air?' she echoed.

He nodded. 'A private helicopter awaits us not far away. It will transport us to our destination. Tell me what we need to do to make your brother's seat secure…'

Distract to divert. The knowledge that he was using boardroom tactics to keep his passenger in line did not impress Anton's sense of fair play, but then, hell, fair play had flown out of the window the moment he'd decided he was not leaving her home without both of them.

She took on the task with focused diligence, placing the baby seat in the gap between the two of them and sliding the spare seat-belt into place. Anton rested his shoulders into the corner of the car and watched, mildly intrigued by the simplistic efficiency of the engineering, while the small baby slept on unaware.

'He is remarkably placid,' he remarked idly.

'He is three weeks old. At this age they sleep, they eat, they sleep again, so long as they are comfortable.' Leaning down, she placed a soft kiss on the boy's button nose.

Her hair spilled over one shoulder as she did so, a shimmering flow of the purest gold he had ever seen. Her hands were nice, he noticed, slender-boned with long, delicately formed fingers and elegant fingernails filed in smooth crescents, unpolished yet shining, not too long, not too short.

'Who is the man in your life?' he asked, curious suddenly because his own attraction to her told him that she must attract them in droves.

Easing back into her own seat, Zoe used one of her hands to smooth her hair back from her cheek before she looked at him. 'Who said there was one?'

'You were locking the back gate after someone's swift exit this morning,' he reminded her. 'I was just curious as to what kind of guy scarpers fast instead of hanging around to offer you support.'

The idea of a heavily pregnant Susie staying around to defend her against this man brought a smile to Zoe's lips. She'd had her share of boyfriends, of course—she was reasonable to look at and popular—but in truth there had never been anyone special in her life, at least not anyone she had felt passionate enough about to lose her head over.

Not that she was about to tell Anton Pallis that. 'I

don't think my personal life is any of your business,' she murmured.

'It is if he's willing to sell the inside story about your personal life.'

He was referring to pillow talk, Zoe realised, and how much information she would have confided to a lover about her family skeletons—namely Theo Kanellis.

'What about the woman in your life?' She threw the question back at him. 'Is she likely to sell her kiss and tell story?'

As a counter response, it earned her a slow smile. 'I don't confide intimate family secrets, and anyway I asked first.'

'Well.' She did not like the way her insides responded to that smile. 'Neither do I. And if there was a man in my life before I climbed into this car with you, then I should imagine he's decided he's been pushed out of the running.'

'Because he knows he can't compete with my fabulous good looks and overall sexy charm?'

He was teasing her, goading her to shoot him down. The problem was that he did have fabulous good looks and loads of sexy charm. 'I was thinking more on the lines of your wealth—and Theo Kanellis's, of course—money giving you both way too much clout for most men to want to try and compete with. However,' she added, 'I will give it to you that you're physical attributes make you a daunting competitor all on your own.'

He laughed out loud this time, low and husky, because he was relaxed so it came from deep within the walls of his chest. Zoe found herself laughing too, softly and ruefully, her eyes connecting with his.

Her first burst of laughter in three long, horrible weeks, she realised suddenly, and then felt guilty because she *could* still laugh.

'So, your turn.' She shifted the attention onto him. 'What about the current woman in your life?'

'I don't have one.'

'That isn't what your press says.'

'The press likes to exaggerate.'

'There was the model in New York three weeks ago,' Zoe recalled. 'She intimated you were both in it for the long haul.'

Anton affected a sigh. 'The problem with women in high-profile careers is they see any kind of press as better than none at all. I broke the relationship off after that interview appeared in the papers.'

'As you mentioned before, *you* are high profile.'

'I am not hankering after a wealthy wife.'

Fair comment, Zoe conceded. 'My father always says—'

She stopped, her lips coming together with a tremulous snap. Turning her face away, she stared blindly at the back of the chauffeur's head and tried to swallow down the new lump in her throat.

'Your father used to say—what?' he prompted very gently.

But Zoe shook her head. The subtle change he'd made to her words didn't stop her from feeling deeply that she'd mentioned her father in the present tense. She did it a lot. She still turned to speak to her mother only to find she wasn't there. She had been going to say that her father had always *said* material wealth did not matter. Love mattered.

'I met him a few times,' Anton said quietly, bringing her face slowly back around so she could look at him. Her eyes looked huge again, and so damned vulnerable. 'I was quite small and he appeared very much a grown-up to me, though he could have been only eighteen. He took me out on the lawn to play football. No one had ever done that with me before…'

Needing to swallow before she could speak, Zoe prompted, 'Your own father?'

'He'd died the year before. I barely remember him. He was always going off somewhere on a business trip and was much too busy being powerful to play football with me. We are here,' he said, sounding as if he was glad of the excuse to call a halt to that line of conversation.

Zoe turned her head in time to watch the front police-car peeling away. The next second the car they were travelling in was slowing down to make a left turn and they were driving through a pair of big gates. Glancing over her shoulder, she saw the two police cars had pulled across the gap into which the gates were in the process of closing behind them. Beyond the police cars the chasing pack had all pulled to a stop in a long line. She could feel their frustration as they climbed out of their vehicles and stared helplessly at their disappearing car. There was even the promised big fence cordoning off the area. Relief skittered down her spine as she turned to look forwards again.

And that feeling of relief died immediately. 'What's going on?' she demanded jerkily.

'Our next mode of transport,' Anton replied.

'But—but that's a plane!'

Taking a look out of the car window at the sleek lines of the Pallis private jet, Anton drawled, 'So it is.'

CHAPTER FOUR

CONFUSED and trying not to let the tiny nub of alarm she could feel inside her start to balloon, Zoe murmured, 'You said a helicopter.'

'A slight change of plan,' Anton countered with the smoothness of balm.

'So we are flying in—that—to your house?'

He watched as his chauffeur climbed out of the car. 'Yes,' he confirmed.

His eyes wore a polished jet look to them that Zoe couldn't read. Having to moisten her lips, she found that they were trembling. 'And wh-where is this house?'

Perhaps she should have asked that question a long time ago. In fact she was angry with herself that she hadn't, because there was something about Anton Pallis now that put her senses on stinging alert. He was still reclining in the corner of the car but she was picking up danger signals that made her reach out with a hand and close it around the handle on Toby's seat.

And he had not answered her question. A new kind of tension sizzled in the air. The chauffeur appeared outside Anton's door and went to open it for him, but with a tap from the back of his fingers on the glass he waved him away without removing his attention from her.

'We are going to Greece, Zoe,' he told her.

'Greece?' She said it as if she had never heard of the place. 'But—but I don't want to go to Greece. And—and you said…'

'I never actually said that my house was here in England,' he pointed out as if she was supposed say, *Oh, that's all right, then. My mistake!*

But Zoe wasn't going to say that. Zoe wasn't going to Greece. 'Not me, Mr Pallis, and not my brother,' she told him on a sudden spurt of movement, and started releasing Toby's seat from its safety restraints.

'So where are you intending to go?' he questioned curiously.

'Back home, where I belong.'

'And how are you going to get there?'

'I will walk if I have to! All the way down that road we've just driven along and straight to the police still hanging around the gate. Or the press,' she added, tight lipped and shaking in her determination to get out of this car as fast as she could. 'Why the heck should I *not* go to the papers and let them decide if this makes you a lying, cheating, kidnapping rat?'

At last he showed some emotion with an impatient hiss from between his even white teeth. 'I may have lied by omission but I am not a cheat and I am *not* kidnapping you.'

She fumbled in her efforts to release the car seat. 'What do you call this then—a holiday?'

'Yes!' he snapped, sitting up out of his corner.

'And who is waiting at the other end of this plane journey, Mr Pallis. Theo Kanellis, by any chance?'

The way she scythed out both names as if they poisoned her to say them set Anton's teeth on edge. 'No,' he denied, then sighed and reached over to clamp a hand on the side of Toby's seat when she tried to pick it up. 'Will you just stop doing that and listen to me?'

'Listen to more of your lies? Do you think I'm an idiot?' She closed both hands over the baby-seat handle. 'You told me to trust you and I did!' she acknowledged bitterly. 'Now look where it's got me!'

'You *can* trust me,' Anton insisted. 'We are *not* going to Theo! On my honour, Zoe, the promise of a sanctuary in my home was the truth.'

And pigs might fly, thought Zoe scornfully. She was forced to let go of Toby's seat with one hand so she could feel behind in search of the door catch so that she could escape. 'I should have known your nice behaviour was fishy,' she said shakily. 'You are *his* loyal representative, after all. No wonder my father steered well clear of you lot, people like you would have eaten a gentle man like him for breakfast and thrown away the bits.'

'This isn't about Leander.'

'Don't you *dare* call him that!' She flared up with spectacular force. 'He is *Mr Ellis* to you. Ellis, because he couldn't stand to use the *Kanellis* name and now I know why—he knew what you were like!'

'I am not a Kanellis, Zoe,' Anton said heavily. 'And this is not what you think. I accept I did not tell you the full truth about where we are going but—'

He ripped out a curse as she began to shiver, all of her shaking like a slender volcano about to erupt, and she'd gone as white as the proverbial sheet.

'Zoe, listen to me— Damn,' he muttered when her door flew open and she began scrambling out of the car.

Anton threw open his door, strode around to her side of the car at speed and reached her side as she turned to bend and collect her brother. Teeth seared together behind his tight lips, he looped an arm around her and hauled her backwards before she could get a firm grip on the baby seat. She wriggled and kicked out at him, he dumped her on the tarmac then spun her around to face him.

'Just listen,' he insisted, half-angry, half-pleading. 'I am sorry I've upset you this badly.'

Upset me? Zoe threw her head back and looked at him. He actually blanched when he saw the electric-blue pools of her eyes spinning his wretched betrayal into the hard angles of his face.

'I hate you,' she choked. 'You duped me all the way! We were safe in our little house. You made it impossible for us to stay there. You, and my grandfather playing your power games. And if you don't let go of me right now, I'm going to start screaming my head off!'

Pulling in a deep breath, she opened her mouth to carry out the threat. Anton's mouth landed on hers with enough power to plug the threatened scream back down her throat. Even he was shocked that he'd used such a method to stop her. Yet once it was done the idea of drawing back again did not enter his head. Her lips were already parted and trembling with tears; he felt their tongues touch and heat explode between them like some unknown, powerful force. She was still sobbing but she kissed him back with hungry urgency. Where it had all come from, he didn't think even she understood.

Across the airfield by the closed gates a line of telescopic cameras lifted in unison to record the kiss. His team of people all stood watching their controlled, sophisticated employer ravish Theo Kanellis's granddaughter, when every one of them knew they'd been embroiled in one hell of a row inside the car only seconds before. And still the passion pulsed between them like a wild, living thing. He held her pressed up against him and the hardening of his body made her choke out a groan in dismay.

Wrenching her lips free from his, she gasped out in quivering rejection, 'That was just gross!'

Anton felt two strikes of heat score across his high cheeks. 'But you still joined in,' he grated back unsteadily—unsteadily because his breathing had gone haywire. He didn't know himself like this.

'You—you—' Zoe ran out of words on a thickened stammer. Her lips felt swollen and hot. Things, senses, were crawling around inside her, aiming stinging strikes at certain intimate parts of her body, from the tightened tips of her crushed breasts to her achingly heavy pelvis where he still held her pressed against the hard evidence of his own response. Even her hair roots were tingling, the long loose strands lying like a splash of gold across one of his shoulders because of the way he had tilted her head.

And the way he was looking down at her, as if he was contemplating kissing her again, shot fear and excitement through Zoe in equal amounts.

'Let go of me,' she breathed into the burning passion stamped onto his handsome face.

No chance, thought Anton. As though he was being driven by some unknown influence, he bent and scooped her into his arms then started walking towards the plane. He felt taut, energised and downright macho. Theo's granddaughter had fast turned into a passionate obsession for him—indefensibly so, he admitted, when those amazing, fascinating eyes flooded with fresh tears again.

'Why are you *doing* this to me?' Zoe sobbed up at him in wretched confusion and pained disbelief.

Then a sound reached her—only the briefest tiniest hint of a squeak—but it was enough to fling Zoe over the edge.

'Toby,' she whispered, and had to strain to look around Anton's broad shoulder. She saw to her horror that the car with its doors still hanging open was already several yards away. 'Anton…Toby. He's still in the— Oh my God, what's that man doing with my baby brother?'

A fresh wave of panic erupted in a swirling spin of dizzying terror. She stared up at the hard cast of his grimly determined face. 'Please,' she begged achingly. 'Don't take my brother away from me!'

Lips clipped tight now, Anton said something to her, but Zoe couldn't hear him over the roaring rush of fear going on in her head. They'd already entered the plane and he was carrying her down the cabin. She knew that she was fighting him, wriggling and hitting out with her clenched fists. 'Toby…' She sobbed out her brother's name over and over, heard it throbbing inside her head.

Lowering her into a seat, Anton came to squat down in front of her. 'Listen to me, Zoe,' he insisted—harshly, because it was only just occurring to him what was actually happening to her. Her eyes had turned black and tears were streaming down her cheeks. Her kiss-crushed lips kept mouthing her brother's name and she was trembling like a leaf.

The muscles in his face clenched tightly and he fixed his attention on fastening her in to her seat. 'Get this plane in the air,' he growled at someone; he didn't give a damn who it was as long as they did what he said.

As if his words had filtered into her head, Zoe's fingers closed around the lapels of his jacket, making him look up, making him feel like the worst person alive when she pleaded, 'Toby, Anton. *Please*, I need my brother. Please, Anton, please…'

It was the agonised cry of a wounded creature. No one was immune to it. Everyone in the cabin froze in dismay, including Anton who had never felt so angry with himself—or so ashamed.

Kostas looked at him as he approached; he was ashamed

of him too. 'Your brother is right here, Miss Kanellis.' The deep slightly thickened voice of Kostas Demitris made Zoe jerk in response. She stopped weeping, blinked her wretched eyes and looked at the seat still holding her baby brother all snug and safe.

'Toby,' she breathed in trembling relief.

'I must secure him in a safety harness while the plane takes off,' continued Kostas in the gentlest voice Anton had ever heard him use, and he'd known the other man for most of his life. 'We will be just up here a couple of seats away. He is safe with me, *thespinis*, I promise you.'

'Thank you,' she whispered, then turned to look at Anton. 'I thought you—'

'I know what you thought,' he cut in grimly. 'For all my faults, Zoe, I promise you I will never hand your brother over to anyone other than to yourself, OK?'

OK? Zoe nodded even though she was asking herself why she was allowing herself to believe a single word that he said. Yet she did.

'He's my whole life now.' Pressing her wobbling lips together, she dropped her gaze to where her fingers still clutched at his jacket lapels. 'He's all I have left of them and…'

Zoe felt the tears well up inside her again, the rolling wave of an overwhelming sadness and grief. For three whole weeks she had kept herself together. She'd stayed calm and strong and kept her feelings all locked up inside because she'd had to if she'd wanted to appear a fit mother for her brother in front of all those people who'd lined up to check her out. Then along came this man—this one person she had actually let her guard down for—and now look at her: stuck on the plane in a middle of a field, waiting to take off for *Greece*!

Anton watched as the tears started flowing again—a

different kind of tears. His lips clamped together and his expression turning tautly blank, he closed his arms around her and used the flat of his hand to ease her face into his chest. He did not offer comforting strokes with his fingers. He did not encourage the tears. He stared at the back of her cream leather seat and just held her as the deep well of her grief opened up and came pouring out. She let go of it all in near silence, in long, soul-wrenching sobs with words, barely distinguishable as words, winding through them. *Mummy* he recognised; *Daddy*...

His flight steward approached him cautiously. 'You need to choose a seat and fasten in, sir,' he said.

Anton shook his head. The plane could fall from the sky but he wasn't moving. After a second or two the steward moved away. The engines fired into life. He felt their vibration through the balls of his balancing feet. The moment they were in the air and free to move around, he unfastened Zoe's belt then stood up with her in his arms and headed for the bedroom at the rear of the plane. Shouldering the door shut behind them, he heeled off his shoes then used a foot to flip away the duvet so he could lay her down on the bed.

She was still clutching his lapels and he did not try to ease her fingers free. He just lay down beside her, flipped the duvet over the two of them then drew her into his embrace. He let her weep those awful sobs against him and felt every single one of them like a blow to his own cruel, thoughtless arrogance. When eventually she exhausted herself and drifted into a restive sleep, he remained where he was, aware with every fibre of his being that he had never held another human being this close to him, and that included during sex.

When slowly her fingers finally relaxed from their grip on him, he eased himself sideways and rolled out of the bed then turned to walk like a drunk into the adjoining bathroom, closed the door and slumped back against it, eyes closed, conscience riven by deserved self-contempt.

Zoe came awake to the slow, slow memory that something calamitous had happened. Shattered images of her shouting at Anton, *kissing* Anton, begging and pleading then weeping on Anton, floated around in her head. She stirred ever so slightly, frowning as she did so because she knew she'd totally embarrassed herself and completely lost her head. Now she was lying in a bed somewhere covered by a duvet and she still had all her clothes on, even her shoes and her jacket.

Unwilling as yet to open her eyes and check out her surroundings, she continued to lie there, using her other senses instead. It was all very quiet. She could feel the finest hint of a vibration from the plane's engines.

Oh dear God, she thought then. She'd had a fight with Anton Pallis about going to Greece then she'd gone to pieces because she'd thought he was separating her from Toby.

'You are awake, then,' a smooth voice said.

With a start, Zoe flipped onto her back then flicked her eyes open as full and detailed recall rushed like a charging bull through her head. She remembered everything—all of it—from her flare of wild panic to…

'I thought you were going to sleep through the whole flight and force me to carry you off it.'

Twisting her head on the pillow, her eyes collided with a pair of dark ones coloured by lazy mockery. Her heart started to hammer. She didn't know why. He was stretched out beside her on top of the duvet with his head supported by the heel of his hand and everything about him screamed sartorial elegance from the grey silk trousers he was wearing now to the crispness of a pale-blue shirt.

'Toby,' she whispered tautly.

'Right here.' Arching an eyebrow as if to question where else her brother could be, he glanced down at the space between them.

And he was. Following the downward movement of Anton's eyes, Zoe discovered her brother lying there fast asleep. He looked relaxed and angelic, his tiny face pink with contentment.

'He drank a full bottle of that awful stuff he seems to find delicious,' Anton informed her. 'Then I tackled a job no man of my superior breeding should ever have to undertake.'

'You fed and changed him?' Turning onto her side, Zoe gathered the baby close to her and dropped a kiss on his silky dark head.

'He suffered my first few fumbling attempts remarkably well. My suit received a—dousing,' he drawled lazily. 'However, since you had already drenched the jacket with your tears earlier, it was no hardship to me to remove it and change into something else.'

He did not add that he had refused plenty of offers from people out there who'd offered to take over the job for him. It had been his punishment to care for the baby, as it was his punishment to endure the frost his staff had been treating him to since he'd walked out of this room over an hour ago.

'I—I don't know what to say,' Zoe mumbled.

'A simple "thank you" will be adequate.'

Not while she still lived and breathed, thought Zoe. 'You don't warrant the waste of good manners. You kidnapped us.'

'Back to hostilities already?' Sighing heavily, he slid off the bed, rising to his full height with fluid grace.

'You lied and you conned me and scared me out of my wits.'

'Well, something made you lose your wits,' Anton agreed, moving across the compact cabin to open a narrow cupboard. 'I did wonder for a while if it was the kiss.'

The moment he mentioned the kiss, Zoe refused to look at him. Her hostility towards him only half-covered what she really felt. 'I suppose I should have expected it from a man reared under Theo Kanellis's influence.' Sitting up in the bed, she lifted her brother into her arms. 'Ruthless, heartless and a calculating bully, as well as a conscience-free rake.'

'You summed me up quite nicely there, Zoe,' Anton agreed again as he slid a jacket off a hanger then closed the cupboard door again. 'Would you like me to apologise for frightening you so badly?'

'Will you turn this plane around to take us back to England?'

In the process of shrugging into his jacket, he paused. 'No.'

She looked up at him when she'd been determined not to. A tight little stabbing feeling skittered down her front. He looked a million dollars again, she saw, and hated him for it because he made her suddenly aware of her own limp, dishevelled state.

'Then your apology has about as much substance as you do as a man of honour.' As soon as she'd said that last word it rang a fuzzy kind of bell in her head.

Frowning, she looked away from him again. But when his steady walk took him across the end of the bed then down along her side of it, she had to flick him a wary glance from beneath her eyelashes to check what he was about to do next.

Anton stopped beside her. She looked like an earth

mother sitting there in a mound of feathery bedding with the boy cradled to her breasts. Only he had never heard of an earth mother with electric-blue eyes, tumbling, golden hair and a soft, pink, pouting mouth that just begged to be—

'If I had been up front and honest with you about bringing you to Greece, would you have agreed to come?'

Pushing her hair away from her face, she shook her head. 'No.'

'Then my honour is intact,' he said. 'You could not stay where you were, and I could not place you anywhere you would have been free from the media circus *except* in Greece, on my private estate.'

'On Theo Kanellis's private island, by any chance?'

'No, and your sarcasm is starting to wear a bit thin on me, Zoe, so be careful. I will accept that my methods were—brutal. And I will acknowledge that you have a right to feel angry and betrayed by me. But that child you cradle in your arms is half-Greek. As are you. He has a right to know his Greek family even if you don't want to know them. Or were you planning on extending the family feud into the next Kanellis generation? If so, then you are no better than the man you refuse to call grandfather. Think about it,' he advised as he turned to stride to the door. 'We land in an hour. Your bag is in the bathroom; I suggest you tidy yourself before you come out of here.'

Zoe glared at his back as he reached to pull the door open. 'Gold-digger,' she muttered.

It froze him where he stood. She hadn't a clue why she'd just blurted that insulting label out, but she felt her pulses pick up pace as he turned around.

The all-powerful Greek tycoon was back, she noticed. She felt tingly and breathless, the one she'd met on her doorstep this morning when he'd stood there looking as if he ruled the world. Every angle of his face was hard, cold and disturbingly immobile—and those eyes had turned back into polished jet.

'You came to my house,' she rushed on with defiance. 'You sweet-talked me into letting you kidnap us. You—you scared me.' As he was doing again now, though she was determined not to show him that. 'For all I know you deliberately agitated the situation with the press because you knew it would work in your favour.'

A spark of self-preservation made her place her brother safely aside then scramble up off the bed. 'What was it your henchman said in my kitchen? *I hope you do know what you're doing, Mr Pallis.*' Zoe quoted word for Greek word. 'Well, you did know, didn't you? Theo wants his grandson and you are going to deliver him even if it means hauling me along too.'

'So how does all of this make me a gold-digger?' He spoke at last, so softly Zoe felt the danger in him like a living thing reaching out towards her with long fingers coming for her throat.

Clenching her hands into fists at her sides, she tried not to be intimidated. 'Everyone knows that until three weeks ago you were Theo's undisputed heir. Then up we pop—Toby and me. Two previously unheard-of grandchildren of the great man himself. You're the lawyer—you tell me how inheritance laws work in Greece. Or, better yet, explain to me again why you've gone to all of this trouble to get us on to this plane going to Greece?'

He was listening with a narrow-eyed intensity that caused a sudden rush of those tremors she'd been trying to hold back. She envied him his self-control in the way he continued to stand there refusing to speak.

'Say something!' she launched at him tautly.

'I am waiting to hear your own conclusions before I comment,' he responded, smooth as silk.

Zoe folded her arms across her front. The way his eyes flickered down to view this piece of screamingly defensive body language made her unfold her arms again and stick them back down at her sides.

'You told me that Theo Kanellis is ill—so ill he can't travel. You told me that he wants my brother and I'm only really along for the ride.'

'I do not recall saying the latter.'

'Yes you did. And, let's face it, causing a huge scandal by walking off with my brother without me would not have done your reputation much good. So why have you gone to all of this trouble? Just to keep your credit sweet with my grandfather?'

She pushed on despite the shrill voice in her head telling her to stop. The man was so still he was dangerous. 'Or do you have more far-reaching plans to do with death, inheritance and baby-boy heirs who will need a mentor? Are you planning to offer my grandfather a deal, whereby you do for Toby what Theo did for you so that you can hang on to control of his fortune and power?'

For a minute she thought he was going to throw back his handsome dark head and laugh at her. In fact there was a quivering part of her that wanted him to do that and turn her 'gold-digger' accusation into a complete joke—but he didn't. Instead he held her pinned to the spot with the hard gleam in his eyes.

'And that is your definition of a gold-digger?' he murmured.

Pressing the tremor out of her lips, Zoe nodded.

'Then you have missed one very salient point—there is a much less *tacky* way for me to keep control of Theo's fortune, and that is through you, Miss Kanellis.'

She didn't like the way that he'd said her name like that. 'I—I don't know what you are talking about.'

'I know you don't.' He started walking towards her. 'Actually I feel rather sad for you that you undervalue your own importance so much.'

'I h-have no importance.' Twenty-two years with no word from her own grandfather had told her that.

'You have a lot of importance,' he insisted. 'You see, I can achieve every one of my gold-digging ambitions by simply making you my wife and taking your brother as my son. Two for the price of one.' He smiled, though it wasn't a nice smile. 'The financier in me loves the sound of that scenario. Why are you staring at me like that?' he questioned ever so curiously. 'You think my sense of honour won't allow me to do it? As we have already established I have no honour. I lie and cheat and kidnap innocents.'

'Stay where you are,' Zoe shot out jerkily.

The gleam in his eyes became a glint like a challenge and he just kept on coming, stalking her backwards like a long, lean hunting-cat.

'But I think your grandfather will be delighted with this marriage plan,' he continued, talking as he stalked. 'Greek men love such sensible business arrangements. They appeal to our macho need to be in control. A merging of our two names would be a formidable coup for me and will send Theo to his grave a very happy man. Now your eyes are flashing a very derisive electric-blue colour as you back away from me,' he observed silkily. 'What is it you fear the most, Miss Kanellis—me, your grandfather…or yourself?'

The final comment made her aware that her heart was racing, that she was breathing fast yet feeling strangled of breath at the same time; that her cheeks had flushed and her lips felt tingly because she could not stop staring at the crazily seductive movement of his mouth as he spoke.

'Perhaps you are thinking that you will not agree to such a deal,' he offered up as an answer for her, his eyes gleaming with mocking humour when her spine hit the bulkhead, leaving her nowhere else to go.

'I have this contingency covered, of course. I will send you to Theo, and he will lock you up until you decide to change your mind. We Greek men are so ruthlessly unscrupulous I might even…'

Reaching up with a hand, he placed the tips of his fingers on the wall right beside her head. 'Kiss you again,' he murmured. 'Bed you,' he added, bringing the lean length of his body closer and closer with each silkily punctuated threat. 'Make you my woman before we even step on to Greek soil and turn you into my—'

Zoe slapped him. She lifted her arm up and crashed the flat of her hand against the side of his face. Her palm stung because his bones were so hard but she didn't care. She'd enjoyed slapping him!

'Get out of my face,' she hissed.

CHAPTER FIVE

HE DID. It actually stunned her when he did exactly that by straightening up and taking a tense step back.

For an endless space of time afterwards, they just stared at each other. The whole ugly scene they'd just enacted hovered between them in a hyperbolic spin of emotions—not all of them of the hostile variety. And that really worried Zoe. Hadn't someone once said that a person in a captive situation can suffer a dangerous attraction for their captor? Well, she was feeling like that right now as she stood with her back flattened to the bulkhead and her legs feeling as if they were about to give way. She was sure that she hated him, but she'd also wanted him to kiss her, and that was the reason why she'd slapped his face—to smash through the frightening allure of her own feelings.

His eyes were like jet again, but burning at their centres with something so terribly intense she knew he could feel the confusion too. He'd gone pale beneath his tanned complexion, a white ring of tension circling the tense compression of his mouth. Her finger marks stood out red on his cheek like a brand and she watched with a trembling mix of defiance and fascination as they slowly faded to white.

When he moved she jumped, wrenching her wary eyes back to his, but all he was doing was releasing a low, grating breath. 'It seems I have succeeded in behaving badly twice in one day,' he acknowledged. 'Please accept my apologies—again.'

Zoe couldn't say anything because her tongue had cleaved to the roof of her mouth. After a shockingly taut few seconds of silence, with a twist of his lips he turned away from her and walked back to the door. It was only after the door closed behind him that Zoe peeled away from the wall and sank weakly down on the bed.

Phew, she thought as she released the pent up breath from her body. She felt like she'd just done ten rounds in a boxing ring—shattered, in other words, limp like a rag. And, what was worse, she was aware that she'd been the one to start that confrontation, goading him on with her 'gold-digger' accusations until he'd reacted.

Why had she done that? Did she really believe that he was a calculating, gold-digging monster prepared to sink to any low depth just to get his hands on her grandfather's power and wealth? Somehow she just did not believe it yet she couldn't work out *why* she did not believe it.

But then, she didn't feel as if she knew anything for a certainty any more. When she'd got up this morning and found the letter from her grandfather lying on the doormat she'd been angry and bitter that he'd dared to write to her at all. When she'd opened her front door to find Anton Pallis standing there, she had been more than ready to take him on. Yet the more they had talked—or sparred, she amended with a quivering grimace—the more she'd begun to like him, instinctively sensing he was someone she could trust.

Did anyone with an ounce of good sense inside them trust a liar? No. So why was she sitting here *wanting* to believe that everything he had just said was just his angry retaliation to her 'gold-digger' charge?

Toby let out a yelp, reminding her that he was there.

Turning to look at him, she smiled when he hiccupped. 'Someone didn't wind you properly,' she told him.

Then she remembered who that someone was: the exotic dark prince who had messed up his Italian-cut suit in his attempts care for her brother while she'd been asleep. She frowned at the pale-blue sleepsuit Toby was wearing, with its studs only half-fastened because the complicated order in which to fasten them had clearly defeated the famously intelligent Anton Pallis.

The dratted man was a disorientating mix of hard and soft, ruthless and sweet. For she did not doubt that he had taken up the task of caring for Toby as an act of penance for the way he'd scared her into a fit of blind, grief-stricken hysterics.

Stretching out across the bed, she rearranged her brother's clothing into order then lifted him onto her shoulder to coax away the hiccups. 'So what do we do, Toby?' she asked him. 'Give in to Mr Hard And Soft and agree to this trip to Greece to meet dear old grandpa? Or do we take the fight with us into the next generation?'

The baby hiccupped again, which was no help, but at least he rid himself of the problem causing them. She laid him back down on the bed. 'Since we are almost *in* Greece, I suppose for now we have to put up and shut up,' she decided heavily.

Then a sudden thought hit her. Greece... Frowning again, Zoe sat up. To enter Greece they needed passports...

Ten minutes later, freshly washed and tidied, Zoe stepped out of the door into the main cabin. As her blue eyes were about to take in the sheer opulence of her luxurious surroundings she'd been too busy panicking to notice before, she was startled into staring at the half-dozen men who rose in unison to their feet.

Lounging comfortably in his own seat, Anton raised

his attention from the laptop he had open on his lap and reviewed this unilateral demonstration of respect from his staff for their passenger. He compared it ruefully to the deep freeze they had been treating him to in silent objection to his driving a grieving young woman to the place into which Zoe had tumbled due to his ruthless method for getting her onto this flight.

Even Kostas wasn't speaking to him. His head of security did not spare him a glance as he passed by his seat on his way to greet Zoe. Returning his gaze to the computer screen, Anton sat in his splendid isolation and listened to Kostas enquiring of Zoe if she had enjoyed a comfortable rest. Polite to an inch, his tough, bulky security chief then offered to settle the boy in the installed flight-bassinette, while the rest of his staff returned to their seats.

He had glimpsed a new side to Kostas Demitris today, Anton mused ruefully, one which had wobbled years of total loyalty to him. Kostas had cornered him the moment he'd stepped out of the bedroom cabin after leaving Zoe to sleep, and he'd told him to his face that he should feel shame for the way he had behaved.

That he did feel shame was something he chose not the share with Kostas. Nor was he going to share the other forces that had been driving him at the time: sex…desire…a dangerous attraction, unwillingly felt but felt all the same. Theo's slender young granddaughter with the vivid eyes, flowing golden hair and pale, pinched vulnerability, stoked up his senses in ways which shocked even him.

That she was prepared to take him on in a fight as if she was his equal only fired him up even more. She had Theo's spunk, though she would be insulted if he told her so. A courageous creature with her life ripped apart, yet valiantly determined to cope. He admired her and lusted after her in equal measures. He'd felt so in tune with her from the moment he'd stepped into her tiny house that he'd failed to question if she would see what he had planned for her and her brother in the same sensible light.

He'd been a man on a mission, focused, driven by the tactical cut and thrust, and so had failed to recognise that she was so fragile the slightest knock to her defences was bound to shatter them. Now he knew he was going to live for a long time with the crucifying sounds of her grief as it poured from her.

His punishment; he deserved it. He even deserved the 'gold-digger' tag, when he still had not bothered to offer up a better side of himself.

Her perfume arrived first, that distinct scent of apple shampoo assailing his nostrils, and he looked up. She had changed her clothes, he noticed, the creased grey dress and black jacket had been replaced by a black tunic that made her skin look startling white and her hair, which she'd brushed away from her face then caught loosely back at her nape, was finer than silk.

'I need to talk to you,' Zoe said, still warily on the defensive but anxious at the same time.

'Of course.' He set the computer aside on the table in front of him. 'Please,' he invited. 'Take a seat.'

He'd removed his jacket again, Zoe noticed, it lay folded on the seat opposite. As he indicated with one of those long brown hands to the chair beside him she bit down into the soft flesh inside her lower lip for a few seconds, not really wanting to sit down so close to him, but too aware of all the other people seemingly dedicated to observing her every move. In the end she sat down on the edge of the chair, so tense her back was ramrod straight.

'You've forgotten something important,' she told him.

'I have?' He frowned as he cast his mind over his meticulous planning.

'Passports.' She nodded. 'Mine is in the box I gave to Kostas to look after, but Toby doesn't have one. You're going to have to turn this plane around because he can't enter Greece without a passport, and I won't have him taken away from me and stuck in some detention centre while I sort out the problem, so—'

'All sorted,' he cut in, feeling curiously pleased with himself that in this one area of concern he had everything covered.

Leaning down to pick something up from the side of his seat, he lifted it onto the table.

Zoe watched in frank bewilderment as he produced a fine leather document-case, set it down then fed back the zip. Sliding out the contents, he sifted through pieces of paper until he came across one bearing the official stamp of a UK government department which he passed across the table to her. Her eyelashes flickered as she looked down at it.

'Your brother is travelling on an emergency visa,' he explained. 'I applied for it on the grounds of your grandfather's ill health.'

While Zoe sat trying to absorb this information, two more pieces of paper arrived beside the first one.

'This one is a letter from your general practitioner saying that Toby is fit to travel, and this one is from Social Services giving you permission to take your brother out of the UK. We—'

'You—you arranged all of this without any of these people applying to me to check if I was OK with it?' Zoe interrupted.

He nodded. 'Mainly as a precaution because of the complications due to probate and your pending legal rights over Toby,' he enlightened her. 'A full passport for Toby will be couriered to you from the British Embassy in Athens in the next few days.'

Zoe was still staring at the accumulation of formal letters lined up in front of her. 'You need a photograph for a passport,' she murmured.

'I took one on my phone and texted it over to the appropriate government body.'

'When did you do that?' she demanded, beginning to simmer inside.

'While you were upstairs packing your things,' was the beautifully modulated response she received. 'With all the press you have been receiving, it needed little explanation for everyone to sympathise with your plight and be eager to fast-track the process. And I know a few useful people.'

He knew a few useful people, Zoe echoed, feeling a nice fresh wave of anger flush up from her chest until it mottled her cheeks. 'Wealth and power have their uses, then.'

He must have heard something in her voice because he turned his dark head. There was a moment of stillness in which he tapped the tips of his fingers against the table and Zoe glared at them as the pressure inside her built and built.

'I'm in trouble again,' he sighed out.

'Where is my input?' she responded tautly.

'I did not need it.' His tone had turned very dry now. 'I put myself up as your attorney, you see.'

'And nobody thought to contact me to check your credibility?'

'As I said—' one of those hands made a rolling gesture '—everyone was very sympathetic and understood that you already had enough on your plate.'

Zoe released a little choked laugh. 'And you are so darned charming and clever at manipulating people, aren't you?'

'I am told it is one of my most annoying traits.'

At last she turned her head to look at him. He was wearing a hint of a smile on his lips and a hint of a rueful apology in his eyes. Sitting back in her seat, she gave a helpless shake of her head. Charm did not even begin to cover what this man was capable of, she thought as she felt her anger die beneath the weight of her incredulity, then felt her own lips being tugged at the corners, wanting to grin.

Sensing an easing in the threatened resurgence of hostilities, Anton caught the eye of his flight steward and brought him striding down the aisle. 'Tea for my guest,' he ordered smoothly. 'And ask Kostas if he will check on the baby. I heard a sound from that direction.'

Nodding, the steward went back down the aisle again. Zoe went to stand up so she could go and check Toby for herself but he covered her hand with his. 'Stay and talk to me,' he said huskily.

She hesitated, which was probably her undoing. It wasn't that she wanted to stay and talk to him—he was the enemy, after all—but those fingers resting on her fingers were gentle, requesting not insisting. She looked down them, saw the difference in his skin, warm and dark against the cool paleness of her own. A now familiar heat flared in her belly, locking her into an argument with herself. She either hated him or she fancied him, but she was sure she couldn't feel both things.

'I am not your enemy, Zoe,' Anton murmured as if he knew exactly what was going on in her head. 'I know I have given you little cause to believe me, but if you will give me the chance I will try my best to amend that.'

She could feel herself wanting to give in. Was it a mild version of Stockholm syndrome? Was she being very stupid here by wanting to believe him again?

Kostas strode past them on his way to check Toby. In a

lightning-flash decision, she stopped him. 'I will go,' she told the security guard, and without allowing herself to glance at Anton she slid her hand out from beneath his, got up and walked away.

They landed as the sun floated low above the glistening sea she'd glimpsed as they'd rushed towards the ground. Kostas, who seemed to have put himself up as her protector, took control of Toby's disembarkation. Zoe didn't brother to argue with him over it.

Everyone was standing up and gathering their things together, including Antõn Pallis, who stood with his back towards her between the table and his seat. He had the most disturbingly beautiful long, muscular back, Zoe found herself noticing, then blinked and made herself stop looking.

The moment the plane shut down its engines he picked up his mobile phone and clamped it to his ear. Zoe heard him start firing out orders like soft bullets, the low growl of his voice a very good substitute to the engines' roar, she thought with a dry smile.

As she was about to draw on her jacket, Kostas said, 'You won't need that, *thespinis*. It is twenty-seven degrees outside.'

Zoe was happy to take the jacket off again since it was now sadly creased after she'd slept in it. A movement just ahead of her in the cabin made her glance up to find that Anton had turned and was looking at her through low hooded eyes. Her chin went up—she didn't know why—like she didn't know why her cheeks started to heat.

They filed out of the plane as if it was any ordinary scheduled flight. Anton was ahead of her and he clearly was not concerned about the heat outside because he'd pulled on his jacket again; the creaseless, elegant businessman was back, she saw as she followed him. Kostas brought up the rear with Toby's seat secure in his big-handed grasp.

At first she paused at the top of the steps to allow the heat to envelope her. It was filled with the most evocative aromas of what she recognised as jasmine, citrus and thyme. Ahead of her on the other side of the shimmering tarmac runway, a line of vehicles waited: two silver limousines, a people carrier and a dusty sedan with an official type standing beside it.

Anton's staff was heading towards him with what she recognised as passports in their hands. Anton followed, with a laptop bag swinging from one broad shoulder. He still had his phone clamped to his ear, his other hand making expressive gestures of irritation as he walked.

Behind Zoe, the hard edge of Toby's seat gave the base of her spine a gentle nudge. She started walking down the shallow flight of steps but there was a strange sensation beginning to swirl inside her legs. She didn't recognise it for what it was until she had taken two strides across the tarmac then she pulled to a trembling stop.

She was in Greece.

Looking down the length of her legs to her shoes, she thought, *I'm standing on the land of my father's birth for the first time in my life.*

Of all the reasons she had been fighting against coming here, this one had never once entered her head, this strange, prickly, stirring sensation which began at her toes and was slowly spreading up her body until it encompassed all of her in the heart-clutching revelation that this moment was the most profound one she'd ever had.

Closing her eyes, she just soaked in the feeling, the strangest impression that she had come home at last. It didn't make sense. She was as British as afternoon tea, as scented roses in the summer, as Big Ben striking the hour with such very British reliability. She was a 'grey cloud and cool climate' girl, a pale blonde with delicate, light skin. She was her mother's daughter, yet she was standing here *feeling* the Greek genes she'd never acknowledged tug themselves free from wherever they'd been hiding and scramble like hungry animals to the surface of her skin.

Tilting her head back, she kept her eyes closed and just took it all in—the sultry heat, the exotic scents, the shimmering gold of the late-afternoon sunlight stroking the back of her eyelids—and she felt strangely at peace.

Was this the reason why her father had never come back here? Because he'd known that he would have to experience the same things she was feeling—this almost spiritual sense of coming home? Home was special. Home was built into the very roots of everyone's psyche. It called to you, drew you to it when you saw it on television—she'd witnessed her father's stillness and seen the shadows cloud his eyes whenever a programme mentioned Greece.

'Zoe…' It was that voice again, the low, dark, modulated voice saying her name like her father had, only this time she recognised the difference.

Lowering her chin, she opened her eyes and found Anton standing in front of her, more handsome, his skin more golden beneath his own sun. His eyes were not polished jet any more but deep, dark warm brown as if they too had been altered by the light. His expression was watchful, and both of his arms were raised in a curve either side of her, but not touching, as if he was waiting to catch her if she fainted away.

'I'm all right,' she whispered.

'You don't look it,' he responded.

'It—it's a bit of a shock to be standing here after all these years,' she admitted. 'I did not expect to—feel anything.'

Anton was beginning to realise that Leander Kanellis's

beautiful daughter felt everything deeply, passionately and with no compromises or restraint. Curiosity as to how all of that passion would translate itself in his arms in his bed fired up his senses, but also had him dropping his arms in an abrupt act of withdrawal.

Forbidden, he told himself. Zoe Kanellis had put herself in forbidden territory the moment she'd accused him of being after her grandfather's money.

His movement brought her into focus with her surroundings for the first time. Everyone else seemed to have disappeared—the dusty sedan, the black people-carrier. Only the two expensive saloons were left standing there.

'I'm sorry,' she murmured. 'I'm holding you up.'

'Not at all,' he responded very politely. 'I have dealt with the necessary formalities. Your brother has not been hauled off to jail.'

'Make a joke of it if it amuses you.' Zoe frowned at him. 'But I was worried.'

'Worry over, then,' he came back smoothly.

'Where is Toby?' she asked then, scanning the two remaining cars for signs of occupation.

'Safe with Kostas in the second car, out of the heat from the sun.' Digging into his jacket pocket, he brought out a maroon leather-bound passport and offered it to her. 'Yours,' he told her. 'Kostas recovered it from your box of papers. I hope it was OK for him to do that.'

Too late if it wasn't, thought Zoe, taking the passport from him with a mumbled, 'Thanks.'

'Then, if you have finished communing with the land of your ancestors, we should leave.'

Drifting out a dry grimace because he almost used the same words she'd been thinking of earlier, Zoe nodded. He turned on his heel and started striding towards the two cars, all brisk, elegant grace and arrogant loftiness that made Zoe pull a wry face as she tagged on behind. She was aware that she'd annoyed him somewhere in the last five minutes though she couldn't work out which bit of their conversation had been the cause.

With a shrug she glanced curiously around her as she walked. They seemed to have landed at yet another private airport which was nothing more than a landing strip with a white-painted concrete observation-tower set high on a plateau of land. She could see the sea glinting in the distance, and the slopes of the pine-coated hills.

'Where are we in Greece, exactly?' she asked curiously.

'This is Thalia.'

She quickened her pace to catch up with him. 'Thalia was the daughter of Zeus,' she said, trying to remember her Greek myths.

'Or the nymph Thalia, deity of rejuvenation?' he suggested. 'No one knows for sure which one the island was named for.'

'This is an island?' The slow rumblings of cold suspicion pulled her to a sudden stop.

Having reached the car, he turned to look at her, his expression growing impatient when he saw her standing still a couple of metres away. 'Can we do the Greek-history lesson another time? It is growing late and I need to be back here in time to take off again before dusk.'

It was like being hit with too much information. Zoe turned a full circle, casting her gaze out across the forest tops. They were surrounded by sea, glinting water everywhere she looked. The island could be no bigger than a few miles wide either way.

'Island,' she whispered, staring at him as if he'd grown horns out of his head. 'You've done it again, haven't you? You've promised me one thing then done something else!'

Looking at her standing there pinned to the shimmering

tarmac in her slender black clothes—which more and more were making him aware that there was a nicely shaped women hidden within—Anton let out a sigh. 'Having a normal conversation with you is like treading on broken glass! What,' he incised, 'Are you getting so fired up about now?'

'This!' Zoe cried, flinging her arms out. 'You are intending to just dump Toby and me here with Theo Kanellis before you fly off into the sunset!'

'Are you out of your head?' Anton fired angrily back at her. 'This is *not* Theo's island it is *my* island! Don't you even know the name of your own father's birthplace?'

The way she blinked those infuriatingly beautiful eyes at him made it clear that she did not. The lowering sun was turning her hair into a halo of spun-golden threads. Oh damn it, he thought, growling the curse inside his own head. And he knew why he was cursing—hell did he know.

'You grandfather's island is called Argiris—*Argiris!*' He repeated it furiously, flinging out one of his arms. 'It lies about fifty kilometres off in that direction.'

'Oh,' she mumbled, and actually swivelled to look as if she had laser vision and could see fifty kilometres away.

He allowed himself the absolutely guilty pleasure of visualising himself striding over there and dragging her into his arms so he could kiss that contrite pout she was now wearing off her pink mouth. 'Get in the car,' he growled, and made do with swinging the car door open then stood, glowering down at his shoes, while he waited for her to come and get into the car.

He caught the scent of her again as she came closer, that distracting smell of freshly cut apples that made the juices inside his mouth spring out on to the flat of his tongue. It attacked other parts of him too, making him pull in the muscles around his hips.

'Blame yourself if I can't trust a single thing that you say or do,' she informed him coolly before she disappeared into the car with an aggravating, lofty flounce.

Anton closed the door with a cringingly gentle click. Zoe bit down on her soft bottom lip and stared after him as he strode off towards the other car. He didn't even want to be in the same car as her any more, she realised, and felt this strange hollow feeling open up in the pit of her stomach.

'It is not always wise to make him angry,' a dry voice murmured beside her.

CHAPTER SIX

STARTLED, Zoe wrenched her head around then blinked when she found Kostas sitting across on the other side of the car with Toby strapped in between them sleeping the sleep of the contented innocent.

'It is not wise to give arrogant bullies like him all their own way, either,' she flicked right back.

'You goad him,' said Kostas.

'I asked him a simple question and he took my head off!' She defended herself despite knowing that she did goad Anton all the time and without really understanding why she needed to do that.

And where was he going to that he needed an extra car? she wondered as she watched the lead car begin to move away. Preferring to slit her own throat than to ask Kostas the question, she made do with telling herself that she didn't care where he was going so long as it was far away from her.

'He has business to attend to in the village.' Kostas, who could clearly read minds, offered up the information without her request. 'He must then be back here to board his plane before sunset arrives because our small airport is not authorised to function after dusk.'

'So this isn't actually his private island, then?' He'd just claimed it as such.

Kostas made a face. 'It is the place of Anton's birth, the home of his late father and many more Pallis fathers before him. Anton built the airport, the small hospital in the village and the new school, and he provides employment for anyone who wants to stay on the island or helps those who prefer to find employment elsewhere.'

There was pride in Kostas's voice as he reeled off his employer's good points, pride and affection. It only stung Zoe's into a stubborn determination to think the worst of Anton Pallis's motives even here in this island where everyone obviously believed he was some kind of living saint. Well, the devil knew how to soften people up with favours—before he demanded your soul as recompense. And she was determined to keep her soul very much intact, thank you very much!

She hated Anton. It was really quite unsettlingly exciting how much she hated him. The feeling kind of taunted her with all different kinds of nerve-stimulating flicks and flurries, so she had to sit tense-backed and consciously control her breathing so what was going on with her on the inside would not show on the outside.

They'd been driving steadily down through the trees since they'd left the tiny airport; now the forest had thinned out to reveal pretty green meadows dotted with olive and fruit groves basking in the sultry late sunlight. In front of them the water was closer, the dusty road they were travelling along showing a junction not far ahead. The front car went to the left; they turned to the right and were suddenly travelling parallel to a pine-edged sandy beach. She could see boats out on the shimmering sea like tiny white dots of glinting white and was surprised to see a small hotel on the opposite side of the road.

'You have a tourist industry here?' she asked because,

despite not wanting to be interested, she discovered that she was.

'Tourism is not discouraged,' said Kostas. 'However it is expected of anyone who comes to stay on Thalia that they maintain standards of behaviour we islanders are used to here.'

Another snippet of information, Zoe acknowledged. Kostas was a native of this island too.

'So, what happens if they don't behave?' Suddenly her lost sense of humour crept out for an airing. 'Does he have them thrown into jail then lord it over them in judgement?'

'He has them removed,' Kostas said, smiling. 'We observe zero tolerance from outsiders here. In a world beset by unruliness and crime we suffer neither. This is the one place Anton can come and relax and simply be himself.'

Wondering what Anton Pallis was like when just 'being himself,' Zoe chose to make no further comment. A despot was still a despot, no matter how relaxed he could make himself. A few minutes later they turned inland again winding around a shallow headland, and then everything changed within the single blink of an eye.

This was sheer heaven tucked in around a pretty crescent-shaped bay. The pine trees marched almost to the edge of the soft sandy beach, which was all she managed to take in before they were turning yet again and she found herself staring at the promised big gates. Though why they were there at all baffled Zoe when she could see no sign of a fence or a wall, just more pine trees forming a shallow wood either side of them.

The gates swung wide to allow the car to drive through them and she forgot all about fences when her vision was suddenly filled the most breathtakingly beautiful white-painted villa, with pale-blue woodwork and a terracotta roof nestling in a gently tended landscape.

Everything was so pretty, she thought as she glanced around her curiously. Nothing was too formal or overstated, just the tall trees forming a majestic backcloth to sun-kissed green lawns and the villa.

The car drew to a stop then in front of a blue-painted door. Zoe turned her attention to releasing her brother's seat from its restraints when Toby suddenly woke up as if some instinct had told him all the hours of travelling were over. He went from sweetly angelic to loudly demanding attention with no gap in between. Abandoning her attempts to release his seat, Zoe swapped to releasing Toby from his safety harness instead, shushing him as she gathered the small protesting baby into her arms before scrambling out of the car.

Kostas was already standing on a deep, shady terrace; his big, bulky frame was being hugged by a small lady with a plump face and shining dark brown eyes.

'This is Anthea, Anton's housekeeper—and my mother.' He introduced Zoe in the gruff voice of embarrassment of a tough guy going all soft in front of his adoring mother. 'This is *thespinis* Kanellis and her brother Toby.' he completed the introductions to his mother who was staring at Zoe with the kind of fascination which made her feel as if she'd just landed here from Mars.

'Beautiful hair.' Anthea sighed out rapturously. 'It is golden like the sun.'

Unsure how to answer that without blushing, Zoe was relieved when Toby notched up his crying levels and grabbed centre stage. The next few minutes went by in a rush as Anthea set about hustling them into the house and up the stairs with Kostas following behind them with their things.

Zoe found herself standing in a pretty room with the sunlight softened by the white drapes across the windows. A huge baby's cot stood in pride of place, with other pieces of baby furniture set efficiently within reach of the cot. She spied a small fridge with en electric kettle placed on top of it, then an old-fashioned rocking chair by the draped window. There was even a television placed comfortably in reach of a small creamy-blue settee. Zoe could tell that the room had been hastily refurbished to accept a small baby, and she suffered a small twist of gratitude towards Anton Pallis because it looked as if he'd tried his best to have the room look as similar as he could to their kitchen in London.

A dark-haired pretty girl the size of a twelve-year-old stepped forward, all shy smiles for Zoe and soothing murmurs of comfort for the weeping boy.

'This is my sister, Martha,' Kostas offered up. 'She is older than she looks. Martha is here to help you with your brother.'

About to insist that she didn't need help with Toby, Zoe bit back on her independent streak when she saw the eager expression on Martha's face. Before she knew it she was handing over the tense, crying bundle of anger that was Toby into Martha's perfectly capable arms.

The next two hours went by in a daze, while between the two of them she and Martha shared soothing the small baby as he went through his usual evening cranky stage. It was gone eight o'clock before she was shown by Anthea into a bedroom directly across the landing from Toby's room.

Decorated in the softest pastel blue, the colour was contrasted by the furniture which was heavy and dark. 'Handmade right here on Thalia,' Anthea informed her proudly. 'Anton prefers to use local craftsmen whenever he can.'

The man could do no wrong, thought Zoe. She walked over to the window to look out on the now pitch darkness and wondered where he was right now—holed up in Athens already, sighing with relief that he'd got away from his irritating charges?

Then Martha wanted to show her the adjoining bathroom and where to find spare toiletries and towels. A few minutes later, Zoe drew open another door next to the bathroom. She did not know what she'd expected to find on the other side of that door but it definitely wasn't the row upon row of beautiful feminine garments, all of them complete strangers to her.

She grew hot, and not just on the outside, imagining one of Anton Pallis's beautiful and sophisticated lovers casually strolling the rails choosing something to wear to please her man, and she backed away from the opening as if the room contained a coven of hissing snakes.

'Anthea, I th-think you've shown me into someone else's bedroom.' She tried to sound casual about it but inside her a strange crashing feeling was taking place.

'No, no, these are for you.' The Greek woman hurried forward to go and stand in the space Zoe had just back away from. 'Anton had them flown out here this afternoon; for he said you had been forced to leave your home so fast it would not occur to you that April is much hotter here than it is in England.'

Dealing with the sinking feeling of relief that she wasn't intruding on someone else's domain, Zoe enquired, 'So, where are my own things?'

'In here too. See?' With a sweeping-arm gesture, Anthea invited her to step forward again. Sure enough, around the edge of the door her things hung or lay neatly folded in a corner looking dark, drab and pathetically few. On closer inspection, as she drifted her eyes over the new clothes, she could see that the style and the fabrics were far more in keeping with a holiday on a Greek island.

For once she did not mock Anton's autocratic belief that

he could just do whatever he wanted to do because he believed he knew best. Nothing here screamed high-fashion designer label at her, though the clothes were of a class way more expensive than the high-street bargains she had only ever been able to afford. And no black amongst them, she noticed, just bright and vibrant primary colours and soft, summery pastels.

Frowning, because she did not like the idea that Anton had been spending money on her she could not afford to pay back, Anthea questioned anxiously, 'You do not like the clothes, *thespinis*?'

Ungrateful and mean-minded, Zoe accused herself, and turned a smile on the Greek woman. 'Of course I like the clothes,' she assured Anthea. 'I'm just finding it—difficult to take in how everyone has gone to so much trouble for Toby and me.'

'Ah.' Anthea flipped her thanks away with the flick of a hand. 'The way those media dogs hung around your doorstep was a disgrace! It is a good thing in my opinion that Anton brought you here, for that kind of thing will not be tolerated on Thalia. Indeed, Anton has gone into town to personally oversee the removal of the reporters who arrived by boat this afternoon. So you relax now,' she advised as she turned to walk across the room. 'You are safe here. Martha will sit with the baby so all you need to do is be comfortable. I will serve dinner in an hour.'

Alone at last, Zoe turned to stare at the bedroom with its big, chunky bed covered in snow-white hand-laced bedding and the rivers of the finest muslin flowing down from the ceiling at the head of the bed. She tried to imagine herself climbing into that bed in her grey cotton pyjamas while clutching a magazine and a mug of hot cocoa as she would do at home. It did not work. Perhaps her thoughtful saviour had covered that pending horror and provided silk nightwear?

She would have to take a look later, but for now… she headed for the bathroom. Forty minutes later—having showered and changed into a white halterneck dress she'd spied on one of the hangers in the dressing room and could not resist trying on—she went to check on Toby and found him blissfully at peace in his huge cot, which made her laugh softly as she leaned over the rail to look at him taking up less than a quarter of the space. Martha was curled up on the sofa surrounded by study books and after a few enquires Zoe discovered the young girl was almost eighteen and swatting for a place at university on the mainland—with Anton's help, of course.

Having left Martha contentedly reading, Zoe wandered down the stairs. She still had ten minutes to kill before it was time for dinner so she used a few of those minutes up taking a look around. Each room she peeped into had a quietly understated style about it which belied the impression she had of Anton Pallis as a sharply modern, outgoing man.

She found the dining room—there were actually two of them—a large, rather grand formal-looking one and this smaller, more intimate room with the circular table already set for its lone diner. Not the most appealing prospect, Zoe mused as she walked along the room towards the pair of long windows she saw standing open at the other end.

Outside on the terrace she paused to glance around. It was so quiet she felt as if she was the only person left in the world. The darkness folded around everything beyond the soft light coming from the house, and the air felt like warm silk each time she breathed it into her lungs. In all of her life she had never experienced quiet like this; it held the true definition of *hush*.

At home she'd been used to the sound of London's never-ending traffic, planes flying into Heathrow, trains rattling past on the track not far away. Even inside the house, quiet was something filled with knocks and bangs and the muffled voices of her neighbours leaking in through the walls either side.

Restless suddenly, she rubbed at her arms with her fingers as she tracked a short way down the terrace, passing beautiful cream-upholstered rattan sofas and chairs set like outside rooms around glass-topped tables. Even out here Anton's home had a quiet elegance about it, she saw. Feeling a sudden breeze pick up, she lifted up her chin to catch hold of its mildly cooling effect.

It was then that she saw them. A *fizz, fizz, fizz* of glorious excitement caught hold of her and she let out a soft gasp of delight. Like someone being invited into fairyland, she ran out into the garden, felt the soft crush of grass beneath her shoes and did not stop until she was standing surrounded by complete darkness. Then and only then did she allow herself to tilt her head again and look up at the wondrous star-studded night sky.

On his way up the path through the trees which led up from the beach, Anton was in no hurry to reach home. This whole day had been one long link of aggravating problems and he was tired and fed up, though watching the boat-load of reporters sail off into the sunset had momentarily cheered him. Hopefully the word would get around to others who fancied trying their luck here that if they so much as stuck a toe over the tidal line they would not enjoy spending hours in the stuffy confines of Thalia's tiny customs office trying to convince a stubbornly deaf officer that they were not a boatful of illegal immigrants attempting to sneak onto the island.

A grim smile touched his lips as he drew towards the end of the path which would give him access onto his front lawn. Milos Loukas could be infuriatingly thorough when he wanted to be. Every passport had to be checked by telephone for its authenticity. Even his own Greek patriots were treated with suspicion and forced to endure the same checks. By the time Anton had arrived on the scene, all six reporters had been more than ready to beg him to get the customs officer off their backs. But it was a case of allowing the official his hour of importance and just taking a back seat until Milos was ready to release them into Anton's care.

Perhaps he should have joined them on their departing boat, he mused, because he'd missed his chance to fly away, which left him with little choice but to come home for the night.

But he did not want to be here. He did not want to suffer the aggravation of another fight with Zoe Kanellis, or worse risk feeding his growing desire…

The sound of a woman's delighted laughter ringing out into the darkness brought his head up and he pulled to a stop. He had decided to delay his arrival here by walking the two miles home from the village via the beach; his eyes had adjusted to the darkness but still he found himself questioning what it was he was staring at.

She looked like the nymph Thalia come out to play while no one was about, a shimmering vision of golden hair and pale, pearlescent skin. The bright white of her dress glowed in the sultry darkness and she stood in the middle of his garden with her face lifted up to the heavens, her beautiful hair spilling down her back.

She was turning slowly as she counted—*counted*—the damn stars up above. Had she gone mad? She was naming them too. He could not hear what names she was saying because her voice was just a breathlessly enchanting whisper, but every couple of seconds another laugh would break from her when she spotted something that truly delighted her.

Standing there on the edge of the path in the shadows, Anton was entranced. He should go; he knew that he should. If anyone was guaranteed to rob all that childlike delight from Zoe Kanellis then it was him. He should just turn around and creep away again like a thief in the night. Go and bunk down on the sofa in Kostas's house in the village. Perhaps the two of them could get drunk on a bottle of ouzo and Kostas could vent his spleen with all the disapproving remarks about Anton's behaviour he had been storing up.

Where had he got the idea that she was too thin?

That dress didn't say thin, it said delicately formed curves in all the right places, the teasing shape of her neat behind and her nipped in little waist. His gaze drifted higher as she completed a full circle, giving him a full-on view of two firmly rounded globes filling the shape of her tie-neck top. The inner growl of his sexual animal brought a soft curse hissing from his lips as his body responded with a flood of fierce heat directly to his pelvis, and he twisted round to face in the opposite direction, intending to make good his escape while he still had the strength.

But he stood on a twig and made it snap. Behind him he heard a sharp little gasp.

'Who is there?' Zoe Kanellis called out uncertainly.

Anton shut his eyes and ground his teeth together. The ensuing silence behind him played across his tense shoulder-muscles and the fine hairs on the back of his neck. If he moved she would see him. If he stayed where he was it was like accepting that he was a scared wimp.

Be a man, Pallis, he told himself, and made himself turn round again.

'I said, who's there?' Zoe repeated, already balancing on the balls of her shoes ready to run. It was so dark over by the trees her eyes were stinging as she tried to pierce through it.

'It's OK,' a familiar voice answered very dryly. 'It is only me.' Her heart gave a giant leap when she saw the tall, lean figure of Anton Pallis emerge from out of the darkness.

'Oh.' She put a hand up to cover the pounding beat of her heart. 'You scared me.'

She caught sight of the way his mouth drew down at the corners in a grimace. He was still wearing the grey suit he'd changed into on the flight over here, only the jacket was no longer on his back put slung over a wide shoulder and held there by a long finger hooked into the loop. His tie had gone, the top few buttons on his shirt dragged open at his taut brown throat. A five o'clock shadow gave his jaw a roguish look and as he came closer she saw how that grimace seemed to mock himself.

'Stargazing, Zoe?' he quizzed.

'I've never seen a sky like it.' She actually smiled at him as she said it, then looked up again as he came to stop a couple of steps away from her. 'It's just glorious.'

'So, how many did you count?'

'I got to two billion before you interrupted.'

'My apologies,' he murmured.

'Accepted,' she returned, softly, because as far as Anton could tell she was busy counting stars again. 'I wish I had my telescope.'

'You have your own telescope?'

'Mmm. If you look just up there—' she raised a pale, slender arm to point towards the night sky '—you can see the dense-star field around the Antares. It's an M4 cluster and looks spectacular here because there's no air pollution to cloud it out.'

Anton looked up and just saw stars. 'Where is this telescope you wish you had with you?'

'I sold it when I left uni… Oh, Anton, look; there's Perseus. How fitting to find him flying over Greece. I could…'

Her excitement faded into nothing when Zoe realised she was talking to a lost audience. He wasn't looking up at the sky, he was watching her with a brooding intensity that flooded a blush into her cheeks.

'Sorry,' she mumbled, her voice turning husky with embarrassment as she added, 'The night sky is my—passion.'

'I can tell,' he said softly.

She was determined not to react to his soft, taunting tone. 'What are you doing here, anyway? I thought you flew off before the sun set.'

'The sun went down and your stars were out before I could get away.'

'The reporters,' Zoe remembered. 'Anthea told me about them. Did you send them packing?'

'Like Zeus, with a single blow of my breath.'

Now he really was mocking her; Zoe stuck up her chin. 'Zeus doesn't have a place up there in the heavens. Up there he's called Jupiter. The Greek gods did not get everything their own way.'

'I know the feeling,' he drawled sardonically.

Meaning she had stopped him getting all his own way? Well, she could argue with that, since she was the one standing here in his garden, on his island, simply because he had decided that this was where she should be.

'So, how did you get here?' She hadn't heard a car while she'd been out here.

'I walked from the village along the beach. I like the dress,' he tagged on casually.

'Oh…thanks.' Looking down at the dress, Zoe started frowning. 'You bought it,' she told him. 'Which is something I need to talk to you about. You should not be spending—'

'Do you like your room?' he interrupted.

'Yes, of course I like my room, it's beautiful. Thank you,' she said again with an added snap of impatience this time. 'But about the clothes…'

'And you found everything you needed to make your brother comfortable?' he cut in on her yet again.

Zoe shifted from one foot to the other. 'That's another thing we need to talk about.' She refused to drop the subject though she knew that what he was trying to make her do. 'All those soft toys and—things—were not necessary. We will only be here for a couple of weeks and Toby is too young to—'

'I believe my staff made you welcome.'

Zoe sucked in some air and clenched her hands into fists. 'You're not going to stop me from telling you what I think, you know!'

'I noticed.' It was his turn to alter his stance. 'However, do you think you could hold back on our next argument until I've at least put a foot inside my house?'

It was the same as a slap on the wrist, Zoe noted, and accepted that she probably deserved it. 'I was just…'

'Shut up now, Zoe,' he urged wearily. 'The clothes were a gift. I will not miss the money. Same thing with the stuffed toys. When I walked out of the wood and first saw you standing here, I was bowled over by how extraordinarily beautiful you looked—until you started sniping at me, then you spoilt it. Now I think I will cut my losses and go inside.'

With that he swung to face the house.

'OK,' she said quickly. 'I accept I should have been more gracious with my thanks.'

Though he didn't walk off, his darkly handsome face with that wicked five o'clock shadow did not look very impressed with her small climb-down.

'It was not my intention to start another fight with you.' Zoe tried again. 'The clothes were a very thoughtful gesture. And I am, truly, very grateful that you went to so much trouble on mine and Toby's behalf and… Well, anyway, I'm sorry I am such an irritant to you and…'

'You are not an irritant,' he clipped out impatiently.

What was she then—warm solicitude?

It was her turn to twitch. 'It really is no use trying to have a normal conversation with you, is it?' She sighed, flicking out a hand in an empty gesture because she didn't like it that her voice had developed a hurt shake. 'I was trying to be *nice*, when you don't deserve it. I must be stark staring mad. After all, even you must know that your behaviour today was pretty much borderline unforgivable.'

Still the stubborn devil held his grim silence. Zoe heaved in a breath.

'However, I am also not stupid. I can see for myself that this place is paradise compared to a small terraced house in Islington laid under siege by the press. But if you believe that you are the only one to have had a horrible day, then—'

He moved so gracefully she didn't see it coming. Next thing he had hold of her chin in the cup of his fingers and a long thumb, and the rest of what she had been about to say just drained from her head. His face was so close to hers now that she could see a brooding restlessness at work behind his darkness, felt a breathless tension spring up between them, made all the more potent by his continuing grim silence.

A slithery, slinky thread of tension began to crawl up her front. If she could she would look away from him because those eyes of his were downright mesmeric and there was something terribly alluring about the stern shape of his lips.

She parted her lips to say something but he gave an infinitesimal shake of his dark head. She knew he was going to kiss her. She could read the dark message of intent plucking at each tiny breath that she took. There was no point by which they were touching other than his light grip on her chin yet the full force of his formidably masculine sensuality still managed to beat over her in waves. The tips of her breasts were tingling, their small, rounded cups filling with the most excruciatingly tender flood of heat. She should move away from him, break the physical connection, but the alarming thing was that she was standing here *waiting* for him to kiss her.

He moved his thumb to run it gently over her bottom lip and the flesh there bloomed with heat. A wry kind of smile softened the grimness from his own mouth as if he knew about the heat and what it meant. Without knowing she was going to do it, she ran the tip of her tongue across the same place, tracking the trail of his thumb. Light flared in his eyes. The air seemed to still, the dome of bright, twinkling stars above them dimmed then darkened altogether. It was just the two of them standing here in the all-consuming darkness trapped by an energy that circled them like a ring.

His expression was so sombre, his gaze so intense, and he towered over her, wide-shouldered, hard-muscled and breathtakingly male. She knew she should be breaking free from this but still she didn't do it. It was appalling and shameful and pride-crushingly weak of her but she just stood there in front of him with her eyes drowning in his eyes and her lips parted, waiting for his kiss.

He murmured something about spellbinding nymphs, then it came, just the lightest touch of his tongue tip against the corner of her mouth and Zoe was startled by the force of pleasure that poured into her blood. Her fingers jerked up to grab hold of his shirt either side of his taut waist. The heat coming from him was stunning, as was the intimacy with which she absorbed his slight intake of breath.

'Ah, Anton, you have arrived at last,' a pleased voice said.

CHAPTER SEVEN

THE two of them sprang apart like guilty lovers caught out enjoying a clandestine tryst. Burning flames licked across Zoe's fair skin as she turned her head and stared dizzily at Anthea, who was standing on the terrace, her rounded shape lit from by the soft light spilling out from the open windows behind her.

Anton sizzled out a curse beneath his breath, released Zoe's chin then stepped around her with the cool swiftness of a man intent on honing the housekeeper's attention onto him. 'Good evening, Anthea,' he greeted smoothly as he strode forward. 'Am I too late for dinner?'

'Of course not,' said the housekeeper. 'Kostas rang to tell me you were walking home along the beach.' The older woman received an affectionate brush of his lips against her cheek. 'How long do you need to shave that prickly beard off your face? Thespinis Kanellis must be starving, for she has not eaten since she arrived.'

'Give me ten minutes to make myself presentable for the dinner table,' she heard Anton say as the two of them walked into the house, leaving Zoe standing alone in the darkness struggling to cool the heat from her face.

I almost ate him, she thought in horror. What did she think she was playing at? What was *he* playing at?

Dragging a large gulp of warm, sultry air into her lungs,

she let it all out again. Being around Anton Pallis was like balancing on a knife edge; she never knew which way she was going to fall off it or whether she was going to cut herself on his sharp edge.

There was nothing sharp about the pulsing throb currently in control of her body; Zoe mocked herself. Right now her lips felt soft and hot, pumped up and trembling with frustrated anticipation. She lifted a hand up to press her fingers against the throb. It just had to stop, she told herself. She had to climb off this crazy emotional swing she was riding on which thrust her from dislike to desire with the lowest point churning into a potent mixture of both.

Dinner turned into a strained affair, with Anton trying his best to make polite conversation and Zoe trying her best to find light responses while Anthea fussed around them like a mother hen.

He offered Zoe wine but she refused, preferring to stick to spring water because she was already feeling intoxicated enough—by him. And her stomach, which had been crying out for sustenance half an hour ago, was now in a state of flux, not wanting to accept the small amount of the delicious creations she did manage to swallow.

Complaining that Zoe did not eat enough to keep a bird alive, the housekeeper removed barely touched dishes and doggedly replaced them with new ones. As soon as the whole ordeal was over, Zoe escaped to bed as soon as she could.

She tried to sleep but she couldn't. She was a churned up, overwrought mess. And it was too quiet. She was used to the sounds of the city serenading her to sleep. The bed was too big and too soft; she was used to being weighted down by a heavy duvet not a couple of starched-white sheets.

And she'd had to leave her bedroom door open, as with Toby's door, because she was afraid she might not hear him when he awoke. What had become an ordinary routine in her own little house felt wrong in this house, as if leaving the door open was like offering an invitation.

Wishful thinking, Zoe? a horrible little voice inside her head taunted her.

'Oh, just shut up,' she told it crossly, tossing over in the bed.

She was actually glad when the first whimpering sounds of her brother wakening filtered over to her bed. Finger-combing her tangled hair as she walked, she padded across the landing and into her brother's room just as his whimpers upped the volume into loud cries for attention.

'OK, OK,' she murmured soothingly, leaning over the cot to lift him out. 'Hungry, hmm?' She smiled down at him as she walked across to the fridge.

Resting Toby in the cradle of one arm, she rocked him while she prepared his bottle, talking softly to him as she did, the routine second nature to her now.

A sound coming from the bedroom doorway made her glance around. 'Oh,' she said.

Anton was standing there wearing a pair of white boxers and a short grey robe he had not bothered to close around the hair-shadowed power in his muscled torso. The fact that she had not bothered to pull on a robe before leaving her bedroom plucked at her senses, making her acutely aware of how she must look.

'He woke me up,' he said, seemingly oblivious to his own state of undress, covering a yawn with the back of his hand. 'Where is Martha? I arranged for her to be here to do the inconvenient stuff.'

'I sent her to bed.' Turning away, Zoe went back to what she had been doing. 'She's swatting for exams and needs her sleep. And taking care of my brother is not inconvenient,' she added, keeping her voice even because Toby had stopped crying and was listening to her with his dark eyes fixed intently on her face. 'I *love* caring for you.' She smiled down at the baby.

One of those silences he was so good at developing filled the space between them. Zoe wished he would go away but he didn't. He just remained where he was, leaning now against the doorframe watching her as she continued with what she was doing with one-handed efficiency.

He'd tied the belt on his robe by the time she turned to walk over to the settee. Studiously ignoring him, she curled up in a corner and settled the baby in her arms with his bottle. At last Anton broke the silence by heaving in a breath and shifting his stance.

'I'm going to make a warm drink, do you want one?'

About to refuse, she realised that her throat felt parched. 'Thank you,' she murmured politely. 'That would be nice.'

He went away and reappeared ten minutes later with a tray containing a china mug filled with what smelled like her favourite, hot chocolate, and another cup containing strong Greek coffee plus a plate with a few home-made cookies on it.

The link Zoe made between the tea and biscuits she'd offered him yesterday morning—was it only yesterday?—put a smile on her lips.

'Enjoy your drink while it's hot. I'll take the baby,' Anton announced, folding down on the other corner of the sofa then holding out an arm and looking at her expectantly.

Zoe wanted to tell him to leave them alone and take his drink with him back to his bed but she did not want to start another round of arguments. With a shrug, she uncoiled enough to hand Toby over then remained poised like that while she waited to see if he knew what he was doing.

He did, of course. The wretched man was a quick learner. He relaxed into his corner of the sofa with her brother comfortably cradled in a big arm and a pair of very tanned legs stretched out in front of him. What piqued Zoe for a second was that Toby made no show of objection. He just wanted his formula no matter who fed it to him, she acknowledged ruefully as she turned to pick up the china mug then filch a cookie before coiling back into her corner.

This was mad.

Who would have believed that she would be sitting here at one o'clock in the morning with Anton Pallis, eating cookies and sipping hot chocolate while he fed a bottle of formula to a small baby boy?

'It's kind of soothing,' he remarked as if he'd been thinking along similar lines. 'He's so small and helpless, he brings out my softer side, the part that makes men want to nurture and protect.'

'Not every man has it.'

'I'm surprised that I have it,' he admitted. 'I had no idea I was a baby kind of man until I had to take care of him on the flight over here.'

'Just think how it would ruin your image if this little scene ever got out.'

'What image?' Dark-brown eyes speared a look at her.

Zoe felt that look all the way down deep into intimate places. 'The ruthless tycoon with his focus concentrated on money and power,' she explained, dipping her eyes so she didn't have to look at him.

Lifting her cup to her mouth, she decided not to mention his equally ruthless reputation with the women he took as lovers then discarded once the novelty had worn off. On paper, a man like that should run a mile in the opposition direction from a scenario like this one.

'Having money and power means you have to be

ruthless, or some other bright spark with his eye on both will strip you clean at the first glimpse of weakness.'

Zoe took a few seconds to think about that then decided that he was probably right. 'Well, a helpless young baby—or a child of any size, for that matter—does not go with that kind of ambition. The desire to nurture and protect gets compromised long the way.'

'Are we talking about Theo and your father now?' he questioned.

Were they? She hadn't thought she was thinking of them when she'd said it. 'Out with the weak one and bring in the stronger one,' she murmured, leaning forward to put down her cup.

And that, Anton noted, was a strike aimed directly at him and his position in Theo's life. 'I am not and I never have been your grandfather's heir, Zoe.' He felt compelled to defend himself.

'No?' She shrugged as if the statement was irrelevant. 'You still spent the last twenty-odd years being honed by him into the person you are now.'

'Is what you are saying that you don't like that person?' Relaxed though he seemed with her brother cradled to his chest, she could see that he was starting to get angry with her.

Even with a glimpse of that anger Zoe was not prepared to hold back what she said next. 'You lied, you cheated and you kidnapped us for a purpose I am still waiting to find out. You tell me what there is there to like.'

'Just this evening you thanked me for kidnapping you,' Anton countered dryly.

'As I also said this evening,' Zoe parried, 'I can appreciate the difference between Islington and here. He's fallen asleep.'

Coolly she shifted the attention back to Toby, slid up off the sofa then bent to take the baby back.

Anton did not try to stop her but, as she carefully eased the sleeping boy from him, their eyes drew level and, without wanting to do it, she glanced up.

It was another one of those moments when everything else just went still, shut down, turned off. His eyes wore a rich dark-brown lustre that spiralled into black and threw her right back into the garden when she'd felt the power of his attraction almost swallow her up. He was so close she could feel his breath feathering her cheekbones, felt a prickling along her nerve ends when he lifted up his hand and gently removed a lock of her hair away from her throat that had slithered forward. Her hands were cupped around the sleeping baby but she was more aware of the backs of her fingers pressing against the hard warmth of Anton's chest. The sexually aroused pulse coming from him beat all around her so she released a stifled little gasp. Heat flooded her bones and she dragged her eyes away from him, ostensibly to concentrate on collecting her brother safely into her arms, but really she knew she was looking away from what was happening between them. The thing that was growing stronger and less easy to break away from each time it happened now.

Anton watched her lift the boy onto her shoulder then straighten up. She was flushed and there was a slight tremor going on in the hand she used to support the baby's back. Aware that he was feeling the heavy drag of desire on his body, he remained where he was, watching her as she began walking up and down while rubbing the boy's back.

He wished he understood this sexual pull he felt for Zoe Kanellis. She should not be his type. He liked his women around his own age with a level of sexual sophistication that saved him having to question if it was good policy to lure them into his bed. But this woman pricked his conscience almost as much as she pricked him in other parts.

And what was she, besides being Theo's granddaughter, that was? She was a twenty-two-year-old bright, beautiful and intelligent straight-A student with the kind of career prospects some would kill to have. She should be scrambling to take the world by storm, yet she'd thrown it all in to care for her brother without a single regret as far as he could tell.

That kind of decision-making required very level-headed maturity, which he admired in her. Or was that part of her the attraction? The novelty of meeting a woman who did not put her own needs before everything, and wasn't selfish or vain, and was so unaware of her own charms that she could walk up and down in a pair of grey cotton pyjamas with a cartoon-character transfer printed on the camisole top?

Then again what those pyjamas did for her figure held a novel appeal in itself. The body inside them moved with a slow, sensual rhythm that highlighted each curve and lithe slender muscle.

'You should go to bed,' Zoe said, wishing he would just get up and go away now.

How did they do it? How did they go from sharing a frankly chilly conversation over a baby's feeding bottle to this, this throbbing physical tension that controlled the very air she drew into her lungs?

She heard him stand up as she bent over the cot to gently place the sleeping baby down in it. As she did so, the tips of her breasts brushed against the rail and she let out a gasp because her nipples were so taut they stung sharply as they grazed the wooden bar.

Oh, please get me out of here! She closed her eyes and sent the prayer winging off into the ether. When eventually she straightened up and turned around, he was waiting for her by the door.

Why?

You know why, she told herself helplessly and started trembling as she made herself walk towards him. She kept her eyes lowered to the floor as she did. They stepped out of Toby's room together. They crossed the landing to her door. It was still swinging open the way she had left it.

'Goodnight, then,' she mumbled, and hated it that the mumble sounded husky and thick.

'One thing,' he said, only pulling to a stop once his shoulder rested against the frame by her head. He was all height and bulk and raw sexuality. 'I will be leaving here in the morning at first light.'

Zoe looked up, caught so off-guard by his announcement she left her expression exposed. It was mad, and she knew it, but she did not want him to go away and leave them.

Anton eased out a sigh. 'It is right that I leave as I promised you I would do,' he murmured. 'Even kidnapping cheats know when it is time to start playing fair.'

He wasn't really talking about what happened yesterday, he was talking about what was happening right here and now. Zoe nodded in agreement but couldn't say anything. A tight band of tension had taken a grip on her throat. Desperate to get away from him before she did or said something really stupid, like begging him not to go, she went to brush past him but he lifted up a hand and stroked a finger down the middle of the cartoon character's famous shape.

'Lucky Snoopy,' he husked.

Zoe sucked in a breath, a thick and trembling shudder of a breath, as all the feelings going haywire inside just lost their final fingernail-grip. Before she knew what she was doing, she had turned towards him again. One look was all that it took; one wide-eyed and helpless electric-blue look and she was raising her arms up to wind them around his shoulders, and leaning towards him, lifting her mouth up. Then she was kissing him like she had been waiting to do it for all of her life.

He actually fought her for a few seconds, lifting his hands up to clasp them around her wrists with the intention of breaking the link she had on him so he could push her away. Maybe she should have let him. Maybe she should have remembered that she didn't even like him and that he was the enemy but she just clung more tightly and leaned into him.

A thick, soft, cursing groan vibrated in his throat. Then he was dropping his hands again so he could close his arms around her and it was Anton who coaxed her lips open wider to indulge in a kiss the likes of which Zoe had never received before.

It was a full, undiluted onslaught of his passionate sensuality that shocked her as much as it excited her.

Just like the heat coming from him, his hard, muscular firmness, the contained power in his arms holding her close. She'd gone from being desperate to see the back of him to so desperate to keep him right here she just clung on. She felt dizzily drunk and confused by so many different emotions but she kissed him back with every ounce of hungry desire that she had. When he speared a set of long fingers into her hair and tilted her head back, the move broke the grip she held on his nape, and her hands slithered around to his front, somehow managing to find their way inside his robe as they did.

His shudder of pleasure as her palms made contact with his skin thrilled her.

Then she wasn't capable of thinking anything because his other hand had slipped beneath her top and was covering her breast. She started trembling, the full force of her attention locked onto those long fingers as they began to stroke and caress. A hot tide of desire swept down through her body. She gasped out feverishly when he grazed her nipple, already standing taut and stinging with the most delicious heat.

She moved restlessly against him, encouraging him with the unknowing instincts of a fledgling siren. The kiss was a drug she wanted to overdose on, as was the feel of his hands stroking slow circles of exploration across her back, her waist, her ribs, then back to her breasts. But, when he clasped her hips to ease her into even closer contact with his body, she felt the power of his arousal with a start of shock that was enough to prize her mouth free.

His eyes were as dark as she'd ever seen them, bands of heat firing across his taut cheeks. 'You're playing with fire, *glikia mou*,' he warned very seriously.

She might have winced or blinked. In truth she no longer knew what she was doing. His lips were still parted, darker and fuller because of the blood pumping into them. She felt the beating pulse of her own swollen lips as she quivered out a small, trembling breath. And that long, hard shaft of male arousal still pressed against her abdomen, causing a wash of moisture to gather between her legs.

Legs that were threatening to break down beneath her.

'So, do we stop?' He tried again, the words arriving from somewhere so deep inside him the question was barely clear enough for her dizzy brain to grasp.

Stop… She picked up from what felt like a long way off. *Stop, let him go, remember exactly who he is.* Rolling her tongue across the pulsing warmth of her lips, she tried to find the strength to give the right answer but it just would not leave her aching throat. His eyes held her eyes, dark and deep and ever so slightly mocking, but she still found herself drowning in them, in the fierce edge of desire she could feel holding every one of his muscles taut. In the end he released a low sound like a laugh, then the muscles in his arms flexed. For a horrible second she thought he was going make the decision for her and put her away from him. In sheer panic, she parted her lips again and whispered, 'I don't want to stop.'

A single flame shot from his eyes and then he was reclaiming her mouth with a deep, sensual fervour that flung the whole thing onto a different level, and he was firing up so many senses it was all she could do just to hang on.

Her hands were buried in his hair now, her body moving to the sensual rhythm of his. Her legs felt so tingly and weak she could barely stand up on them and, as if he recognised the problem, he bent and scooped her up against her chest.

The kiss did not break as he crossed her bedroom; it still clung when he set her down beside the bed. She didn't notice the efficient way he dispensed with his robe and her top—not until she felt the coolness of cotton against her back. She opened her eyes in time to soak in the sheer masculine beauty of his naked bronzed torso as he lowered himself down beside her then drew her back into his arms.

'Anton…' she whispered, and did not know why she was whispering his name like that.

He seemed to understand, though, because he fed out unevenly, 'I know,' and stroked his hand down the flat surface of her front then beneath her pyjama bottoms, sending shockwaves of taut, tingling sensation skimming across her flesh.

She cried out, in no control of the way her hips arched up towards those seeking fingers. He caught her up to him and completed the smooth, invading stroke into the pool of moist heat and watched her as she just went wild. Her heartbeat thundered out of control as his tongue darted into her mouth and began a sensual mimicking of what his fingers were doing to her while she clutched at his shoulders and shook.

He was hot and hard and felt like satin. Every sensitised nerve in her body craved his attention; every glide of his fingers, every touch with his mouth, drove her deeper and deeper into a yawning black chasm filled with sparkling, bright starbursts of blinding light. She writhed and quivered and he kissed her so deeply and so often that she never got the chance to even think of pulling back from the brink.

The trail of his fingers dipped into that molten place and sent her twisting restlessly onto her side, her limbs curling upwards in a roll of ecstasy. He muttered something and gently straightened her out again, trailing away her final piece of clothing, then deepening that limb-curling caress until she was sobbing his name out again and again. She vaguely noticed that there was a raw, trembling urgency vibrating behind the determined patience with which he was arousing her, higher and higher, until she wondered if she was going to pass out through lack of oxygen getting through to her lungs.

Although she was breathing in short, frantic gasps she did not feel she was gaining anything from it.

But all of that raw-edged patience fled when she touched him. Her restless fingers brushed against him by accident at first, then not by accident when she discovered the thick velvet beauty of his long, swollen length. He captured her wrist and drew her hand away, shuddering as he did so, and cursing softly as he pushed her flat then rolled on top of her, overwhelming every inch of her slender frame with his stronger, harder more powerful body.

He let her feel his weight, the sweat-slicked heated tremors of his pleasure. Her breasts were crushed against hair-roughened hot skin, their distended tips so sensitised she could barely stand the aggressive rasp. When he let go of her wrist, she wrapped her arm around his shoulders, not thinking of anything else but the aching need for more of what he was making her feel.

His mouth did not leave her mouth, not once, keeping her so sunk down in the swirling mists it did not occur to her what was going to come next until it was too late. He settled his hips between her spread thighs and she felt for the first time the probe of his manhood nudge against the tender heart of her sex just a short, blinding second before he drove inside, forging his route like a conquering warrior claiming his prize.

It was too late for her to warn him as the screaming shock of sudden agony split through her like forked lightning, arching her spine and clenching her muscles on a high-pitched, pained cry.

Anton froze like a man turned to marble. He stared down at her as she flicked open her eyes. Bright, spearing sparks of vivid blue attacked his shock like piercing pin-pricks. He had never felt so totally shattered about anything in his entire life.

'No,' he ground out unsteadily.

Zoe couldn't say anything; she was feeling so very shattered herself. His full pulsing length was buried inside her, no thought to hold back any of it, no compromise at all. And her muscles were working along him like some hot, bloody torment.

'You cannot be,' he ground into her shock-whitened face.

'I hate you,' she choked, then she cried out again for a completely different reason when he tried to withdraw. 'Don't you dare—don't you *dare*!' she gasped then. 'Oh God,' she groaned when he stilled instantly, severe tension scoring his face. 'I hate you,' she moaned out a second time. 'You did not deserve this but I want you—I *want* you!'

Reaching up, he pushed her damp, tangled hair away from her face. His fingers were trembling, Zoe noticed. Remorse glittered in the heavy darkness of his eyes. But when he made a gentle move with his hips it wasn't pain that made Zoe writhe and quiver, and the remorse in him turned into desire as he set a hot, sensual rhythm that lost her in layer upon layer of erotic excitement. Her eyes clung to his with an intensity which heightened the whole experience. He kept kissing the increasingly more helpless gasps from her lips.

'Anton,' she kept on breathing his name and each time she said it his rhythm grew fiercer, as if hearing her chant his name fed his fire.

When she felt herself reaching a vital pinnacle between this moment and what was about to happen, he buried his fingers in her hair and gave her the full, devouring force of his kiss. She tipped, she cried out, she clung to his shoulders as she tumbled, she fell apart beneath him and all around him, and finally experienced the dizzy pleasure of feeling him fall apart with her.

The flowing river of release she was floating down barely lasted a minute before he was ruining it, grating out a word in Greek that made her jerk in startled dismay. Her eyes flew open. She found him glaring down at her, the next second he was levering himself up and throwing himself to his feet by the bed.

Totally gloriously magnificent in his nakedness, he stood like he'd been turned into a bronze statue, the potency of his sex still a powerful thing to behold, which surprised Zoe; she had no previous experience to call upon to know if this was normal.

Curling up onto her side, she waited in the pulsing

silence for what she knew was coming next. She should have told him. She'd known that even while she could use the excuse that the passion had just taken her over. She'd kept quiet, though for reasons she was not ready quite to face yet. And her body was still busy indulging in the aftermath, the pounding beat of her heart refusing to ease. Down between her thighs, the new pulse point he had encouraged was still busy beating out a soft tattoo of lingering pleasure, the muscles inside her emitting tender little aches and quivers as they took their time settling back into their usual place.

But the beat of his anger rode over everything. It bounded off the walls and the tense stillness of his naked frame. He wasn't looking at her—he hadn't looked at her properly since they had tumbled into that totally mutual high-octane orgasm. He was staring at nothing, as far as she could see.

'I knew what I was doing,' she said; better late than never, she supposed.

The sound of her voice sprang him out from behind the locked door holding him so still. With a flaring blast of energy, he spun around, spied his boxers lying on the floor and bent to snatch them up. His anger crackled in every sharp movement as he dragged them on up his long legs then the taut contours of his golden flanks.

'If you did, then I am ashamed of you,' he incised so cleanly she was surprised the words didn't draw blood.

CHAPTER EIGHT

IN THE process of dragging out the crumpled sheet from beneath her naked body so she could cover herself with it, Zoe went still.

He was ashamed of her?

'It is not your place to be ashamed of me.' Yanking out the sheet she pinned it tight across her breasts. 'You are my captor not the keeper of my morals. Look after your own morals, Anton, since they have more sins to answer than mine do.'

'I can't believe I fell for this,' he muttered, having turned himself back into a statue again.

'Fell for what?' Pulling herself up against the pillows, Zoe stared at him in growing anger.

'You and your clever bit of reverse psychology,' he enlightened her. 'You accused *me* of being a manipulating gold-digger, when all the time you've been busy plotting how best to protect your own interests!'

'You've lost me,' Zoe told him. 'Where,' she demanded, 'In what just happened between us, was I protecting my own interests?'

'You were a virgin.'

Flushing to the roots of her tumbled hair, she peeled out sarcastically, 'Oh, thanks for reminding me. I forgot.'

'You are Theo Kanellis's granddaughter.'

'Just another unfortunate truth I would much rather not be reminded of.'

'If you wanted to stick a knife through my relationship with Theo, you could not have come up with a better way of doing it.'

'That's one Machiavellian conversation you've got going with yourself there,' said Zoe, picking up a spare pillow from the bed and hugging it tightly to her front. 'Tell me, how does it work that me having sex with you sticks a knife in your relationship with Theo?'

'You were a virgin.'

'Will you *stop* saying that?' Zoe launched at him, trembling in disgust.

At last he turned to look at her, his proud dark head thrown back. His nostrils flared as he took in some air, contempt spilling from his polished jet eyes onto her hot embarrassed face. 'You were a *virgin*!' he repeated like it was the vilest swearword. 'Now I will have to marry you before Theo finds out what I have done!'

Marry her? Beginning to feel as if she was stuck in one of those living nightmares which never ever made any sense, Zoe stared at the spectre playing the starring role. She would not have been surprised if he'd grown horns and hooves. He had the body of a Greek god and the mind of a convoluted madman. And the hard, arrogant and beautiful face of a prince of darkness.

Shuddering inside the sheet at her own crazed imagination, she hugged the pillow all the tighter. 'I am not about to confess to him that I let you do this to me,' she assured him icily. 'I mean, why would I want to? You were right, by the way. I am now *very* ashamed of myself.'

'You are deliberately not following me.' He sounded oddly strained suddenly. Glancing up, Zoe tracked where he was looking and realised the sheet was not covering a creamy hip and a long thigh.

Yanking the sheet into place, she decided to say nothing. It was useless to try anyway because she could feel hot tears beginning to build in her eyes and her throat burn.

'In all honour, *I* will have to tell him. So you've won, Miss Kanellis. You have damned me in your grandfather's eyes and protected your inheritance!'

'In all *honour*?' Zoe forced past the tears. 'How dare you talk to me about your honour? You don't have any honour!' Hanging on to the pillow she scrambled off the bed because she could no longer sit there while he spilled his disgust out all over her.

'Twenty-four hours ago you were a stranger to me—just the the *substitute son* standing in place of my father with your lofty head stuck into Theo's billions, while Toby and I hid away like sewer rats from *your* sleazy press! I have just lost both of m-my parents.' Her voice thickened and wavered as the tears momentarily won out. She pulled in a strained, unsteady lungful of air.

'Did you care about that when you turned up on our doorstep? No. You just doubled the press hype without a care because it was more important that you jumped and danced to m-my grandfather's tune in an effort to protect your own position in his life!'

'Zoe…'

'Shut up!' she whipped out thickly, too upset now to see the pallor currently robbing his face of its tan. 'You've had your say, now it's my turn! I will repeat this very clearly and will even have it written down and sign it in triplicate if you like: *I do not want my grandfather's money!* So you're safe, Mr Pallis—safe from me, from marriage and from any other rotten thing you feel like throwing at me!'

It was only when she felt his fingers tremble slightly

as he brushed a tear from her cheek that she realised he'd moved in that close. She stepped back, raising up the pillow to swipe the tears away for herself.

'I thought that we had both just lost control tonight, but…' she mumbled.

'We did.'

She turned her back on that one, having forgotten that she was wearing nothing but the pillow, unaware that Anton was clenching his teeth, his jaw and his fists in an effort not to reach for the sheet to cover her up. It felt so wrong to further embarrass her. He had done enough. He wished he knew what had been driving him to say all of those things because, now that sanity had returned to him, he knew he had been spouting a load of rubbish.

'I thought it was kind of inevitable—the way we've been sparking off each other all day.'

'It was,' Anton husked, then gave in to the need to protect her dignity and reached for the sheet, carefully dropping it across her trembling shoulders. 'You're so cold you're shivering,' he used for an excuse.

Zoe grabbed the flowing edges of the white cotton and hugged them to her, then spun around.

Her eyes glistened vivid blue in the pale oval of her face and he didn't know what to say to her to put right what he'd just done. 'I am sorry I reacted so—badly,' seemed totally inadequate when he thought back over what he had accused her of. 'It was just that—'

'You're worried because you've just had sex with Theo's granddaughter,' she finished for him.

'I don't give a damn about who you are!' He sighed impatiently. 'I don't even know why I said it. But if you had only told me you were a—'

'Get out,' Zoe said because she didn't want to listen to him using that word again. 'If I have one small say in this *horrible* situation you've placed me in, then it's the right to my own privacy in this room, so please, just get *out*!'

Spinning away again, she stood trembling inside the tight wrap of the sheet, aware that she was about to lose complete control and fall into a flood of weeping the likes of which would beat the one she'd fallen into on his stupid plane.

'We both lost our heads.' Still he persisted doggedly. 'I did not expect… I feel so guilty!' he said roughly. 'I could have made the experience less uncomfortable for you but instead we went into it like…'

At last he ran out of words and Zoe was glad that he did. She did not need a running commentary on what they had done, or the way that they had done it. 'Please,' she begged him. 'Will you just get out?'

'We will talk tomorrow,' he said finally, turning towards the door.

'You're flying off in the morning to—somewhere,' she reminded him and hoped to goodness it was far, far away.

'I don't think so,' he returned. 'We need to—'

'You are flying off tomorrow,' Zoe repeated. 'Because you promised me you would leave me alone in peace here for two weeks then allow me to go home—and I am insisting you keep those promises at least.'

Maybe he nodded in agreement. She had her back to him so she would not know. Yet somehow she knew that his lengthening silence was an agreement to her wishes. *In all honour* he could do little else.

Anton's plane took off at sunrise. He had not been to bed. If he'd ever wanted to know how Leander Kanellis had felt when he'd been expelled from his home and family, then he knew now.

Two weeks… He had promised Zoe a two-week sanctuary

and hell would have to freeze over before he would allow himself to break that promise now. Leaning back in his seat, he closed his weary eyes. Sleep deprivation was not a malady he usually suffered from but he was feeling the dragging pinch of it right now.

Or maybe it was the fault of the amount of brandy he had consumed while he'd sat in a chair in his bedroom with his feet up on the windowsill, drowning his restless sorrows while playing back gut-grinding snatches of what had turned out to be the most mind-blowing experience of his long sexual history.

Great sex, lousy aftermath. He shifted his shoulders against the cream leather back of his seat. He did not need to replay the way he'd laid into her in an effort to salve his own guilty conscience.

Women… He blamed all those other women who'd drifted in and out of his bed with their third eye focused on the vague chance that they might—just might—be the one he would decide to marry. And not merely for his handsome self; he mocked the good looks he was not too modest to acknowledge he had been blessed with. Or even his famous prowess between the sheets. No, money was the drug they fell in love with, the scintillating lure of becoming Mrs Anton Pallis with all the wealth, power and position the title would bring along with it.

So he'd become cynical about women before he'd reached the age of twenty. So he'd taken what they'd invited him to take, enjoyed their company and their bodies for as long as his interest lasted and never thought much about how it must feel to be in their shoes.

Well, he was feeling it now: rejection. In this case, a well-deserved rejection. The low ache of knowing he had been pushed out into the cold when, for the first time in his life, he'd wanted to stay in the warm. Somehow yesterday

Zoe Kanellis had wriggled her way past his usual guard. He even liked the baby. He'd got up from his chair at four-thirty this morning and rushed to pick the boy up when he'd cried. That Zoe had not come running into the boy's room as well had surprised him, until he'd glanced across the landing and seen that her door was closed.

He had done that. He had closed her bedroom door on his way out of it, and she had been too upset to notice that he had. So he'd done his one good deed for this day and dealt with the baby's needs without disturbing anyone else.

'Anton?'

'Hmm?' he grunted, frowning because he did not want to be disturbed.

'Fresh trouble,' Kostas warned him grimly.

Zoe guided the buggy along one of the shady pathways which meandered through the garden. It was strange to think that this was Toby's first taste of fresh air since she'd brought him home from the hospital.

The good side of her bolthole in paradise, she thought grimly. The serpent had flown out this morning—or so she'd been informed. She'd been out for the count when Anton had left here, having thrown herself back on the bed and buried her head between two pillows in an effort to hide away from what they had done.

A glint of light in the corner of her eye made her turn her head to see a silver Mercedes sweep in through the gates situated over on the other side of the garden. She froze. Surely he could not have come back? He would not come back. The man she'd been faced with after their senseless, wild frolic in her bed would clip his own wings off before he would come back here before the two promised weeks were up.

If even then, she added as she turned away to continue

walking while shuddering inside now that the memories of last night's horror had resurfaced. And it wasn't even his behaviour that was making her shudder. No, it was her own. She hated herself. She hated him. He'd told her she should be ashamed of herself and she was. Though what his conscience had been telling him to feel had got lost in the bitterness that poured forth from his angry lips.

Guilty he'd admitted to, but only when it had been dragged out of him. Well, great. She was his guilty sin, because she would have to have been totally naive and stupid not to notice that he'd had the hots for her almost from the first moment he looked at her.

And you for him, that little voice in her head called honesty chimed in.

Zoe lifted and dropped her tense narrow shoulders as if trying to shrug honesty away. She was a twenty-two-year-old, reasonably attractive woman who'd been batting off the attentions of the opposite sex since she'd suddenly grown breasts and long legs at the age of fourteen. She was a self-confessed swat, a classic blue stocking who would rather spend her time battling with some complicated calculus than flirting with her peers. Her father used to laugh at the clutch of doe-eyed boys who'd used to loiter outside their house waiting for her to walk out of the door.

'You don't feel a thing for them, do you?' His amused voice echoed inside her head and she had to blink the glaze of tears from her eyes.

She had been a late developer. He'd been proud of her blossoming beauty and kind of relieved at the same time that she wasn't seduced by the pubescent yearnings of her followers. She'd sailed through the coming years of her slow adolescent development and come out of it the other end with any sudden waves of sexually hormonal rushes tempered by good old-fashioned common sense.

Good old-fashioned common sense… Zoe mocked the phrase which had been her uni mantra. She'd been friendly and popular but her compatriots had used to tease her for her level-headed approach to sex and the tumult of excitement that went along with it. They would probably laugh themselves silly if they could see her now, seduced and well bedded by a notorious womanizer within twenty-four hours of meeting him for the first time.

Knocked off her sensible pedestal. Tumbled by the darkly handsome Greek who was a dangerous mix of cold-blooded ruthlessness and annihilating charm.

The sound of hurried steps behind her made Zoe stop and turn. Martha was coming down the path towards her, her pretty face anxious. What now? Zoe thought wearily as she waited for the other girl to catch up with her.

'Anton sent me to find you, *thespinis*,' Martha explained as she came close. 'He requests that you will please go to him in his study.'

'You mean he's here, at the house?' Zoe started, frowning. 'But I thought—'

'He flew to Athens this morning but now he is back,' explained Martha as if it was nothing unusual to her that Anton should shunt himself about the Aegean like a number fifty-two bus.

Martha waved a hand at Toby's buggy. 'I am to take care of the little one while you go.'

Relinquishing Toby into Martha's care, Zoe walked back up the path towards the house. She tried to come up with a good enough reason that would bring him back here this fast, but couldn't think of a single thing.

The door to his study stood open by a couple of inches. Still, she knocked lightly on the wood before she pushed it open that little bit wider and stepped warily through the gap. She'd peeped into this room during her quick exploration of the downstairs yesterday, so she remembered its basic layout which consisted of loads of honey-coloured book shelves and furniture, a big fireplace filled with unlit logs, a black leather sofa, a couple of matching chairs and a desk, behind which Anton was standing right now.

He was the lofty tycoon again, she saw with a sinking feeling. A tall, dark power-force of a man wearing an eye-poppingly elegant black silk suit with a fine white stripe running through it that made her think of hard-headed City types. She felt consumed suddenly by an unfamiliar urge to check out her hair and run her palms down the side of the pale-blue straight cotton skirt she'd put on this morning. He looked up and she went still, stricken by a sudden leap of feeling which made her hot with horrible awareness.

'You asked to see me.' She fought to keep her voice cool and level.

It was then that she saw his grim-faced expression, the formality with which he nodded. A shiver of alarm took care of the other hotter feelings, consigning them to the archives of her mind—where she preferred them to stay.

'So what's gone wrong now?' she asked as she walked towards the desk.

She'd had too many bad shocks recently not to recognise when another one was on its way.

'You need to see this.' He waved a hand at something lying flat on the desk, Zoe looked down with caution.

It was a newspaper, she saw. A British tabloid conveniently placed to face in her direction so she didn't have to strain her neck to see what was printed on it.

Pallis Crushes Opposition! the headline read.

Snatching the paper up, she just stared at the accompanying photographs until her hands started to shake. The totally humiliating sight of Anton carrying her onto the plane was bad enough, but to see the two of them captured in stark black-and-white, standing by the car locked in a passionate embrace, dropped her like a stone onto a nearby chair. Her face burned hot then paled in crushing mortification. They looked as if it would need a crowbar to prize them apart. The article below read:

> In a nifty move that left us all gasping yesterday, Greek tycoon Anton Pallis closed in on the new Kanellis heiress with a speed that left us in no doubt as to where the future prospects of the Kanellis fortune lie. If he's not going to get the money by deed of succession, he's determined to get control of it another way. If that means taking control of Zoe Kanellis at the same time, then why not? She's young, she's beautiful and, as the hot clinch shows, she's already fallen for the handsome Greek to the point he had to carry her onto their flight to Greece. Next step wedding bells? Well, business is business, after all.

'So much for you protecting us,' Zoe whispered finally, while he continued to stand there like the grim reaper, doing and saying nothing at all. 'Even *they* think you are a gold-digger.'

'So it would seem,' he responded impassively.

'While I'm the brainless blonde bimbo who falls into your arms like a ripe plum.' Impassive did not do it for Zoe; in sheer, angry frustration she ripped the page out of the newspaper with tight trembling fingers then screwed it into a tight ball and stood up, full of intent.

'I wouldn't if I were you,' Anton drawled. 'I will allow you to be angry with me and with them.' He flicked a glance at her clenched fist. 'Hurling missiles at me, however, is likely to earn a response.'

'But this is all your fault!' She hurled a verbal missile at him instead, the newspaper page still crushed in her fist while the rest of the rag lay in a spread of pages at her feet. 'If you hadn't—'

'Kissed you?'

'*Kidnapped* me and Toby. None of this would have happened!'

'I love it that I seem to be the only one who lost their head in that clinch, *agape mou*,' he said dryly. 'While you were beating me off with a large stick, of course.'

Zoe remembered the kiss then. The hot, hungry urgency with which she'd fallen into it, the way she'd clung to him. 'I was hysterical.'

'Or something.'

'I was hysterical!' she repeated furiously. 'You took advantage! In fact, you haven't stopped taking advantage of me since you forced your way in through my front door.'

'Forced? I recall no use of force.'

'Well, you wouldn't, being so damned arrogant,' she muttered, turning away from his annoyingly controlled stance. 'So what happens next?' She instantly turned back to lance at him. 'Do you deny all charges and demand a retraction and an apology?'

'Dear God, no. That would only make the story run on.'

'Then why have you come back here to face me with this?' She would have been much happier left in blind ignorance.

'Because your grandfather has seen the article,' he said with such laconic calm Zoe shot up her chin to stare at him, only to realise her big mistake.

Until that second she had been studiously *not* looking directly into his face. It had been a case of plain and simple self-defence. Having to come in here and deal with the man she had all but begged to make love to her the night before had taken courage, in the form of mental blindness like he was an out-of-focus shape lurking in the shadows.

Only he wasn't in the shadows. He was standing with the morning sun streaming in through the window to one side of him, throwing his staggering physical attraction into totally unfair relief: the black hair, the dark suit, the clean shaven skin. His overwhelming height and that other vital ingredient that made her lungs feel hot and her throat close up as she took it in—his sexuality, made all the more raw and rampant now that it was cloaked in all the daunting sophistication of his clothes and the impassive mask he had in place.

But she'd seen him naked. She'd felt him tremble in her arms. She knew how it felt to have him deep inside her and she'd witnessed how *he* felt when he'd lost all of that cool civility to the wild throws of orgasmic relief.

Heat flooded up her neck and into her cheekbones; she had a horrible feeling her eyes had turned black. He was stunningly, staggeringly beautiful. Even the sun loved him so much she found herself wondering how he would look standing there with no clothes on.

'So, why should that be of interest to me?' She threw the words at him, loaded down with an angst that came directly from what she was fighting against inside herself.

He arched a black satin eyebrow. 'Even you cannot be that indifferent to a sick old man's feelings.'

'I don't understand why he should have any feelings about the article one way or another,' Zoe responded. 'It isn't any of his business what we were doing.'

He narrowed his eyes, and Zoe felt that awful fizz of awareness tingle her skin. He knew what she had been thinking a moment ago, she was sure of it.

'At least you admit you were doing it too,' was all that he said.

Unable to deny it, Zoe made herself stay silent. It was tougher though to make herself remain still when he decided to stride around the desk then squat down to gather up the rest of the newspaper where it lay on the floor after sliding off her lap when she'd jumped to her feet. The paper collected up, he rose to his full height again and placed it on the desk. When he reached out and took hold of her clenched fist, she almost bit through her tongue in an effort to control the urge not to jerk back from him.

Gently prising open her fingers, he took the balled-up sheet of newspaper from her and tossed it onto the desk as well. 'OK,' he said, still holding her hand. 'If the histrionics are over, let's see if we can talk this through calmly like adults.'

The implication that she was behaving like a child did not go down well, especially when Zoe knew it was partially the truth. 'I don't want to discuss my grandfather,' she stated, trying to inch her hand back without it looking like she was desperate to do it.

'However, I do,' Anton countered. 'But first, tell me how you are feeling today.'

That made her snatch her hand back. It also drove all the heat back into her cheeks. 'If you're referring to last night, then please don't bother. I'm fine. You're fine.' She turned around and started walking for the door. 'I will leave you to deal with Theo,' she announced over her shoulder.

'Are you absolutely sure you want me to do that?' he asked.

'Yes.' Zoe gave a firm nod as she reached for the door knob.

'Right,' Anton said as she pulled the door open. 'We will be married here on this island next week, then.'

CHAPTER NINE

ZOE froze like a statue. She didn't breathe or blink.

'In truth, I confess that I'm relieved you are being so sensible about this. I expected one hell of a fight from you, but I am not about to spoil the moment. It is so good to know you are willing to trust me again.'

His smoothly delivered speech hinted only at sarcasm, but it still slid like a shiver down her spine. Zoe slowly closed the door again. When she turned round to face him he was lounging back against the desk, elegant jacket elbowed back from his elegant shirt, elegant hands resting in his trouser pockets, elegant long legs stretched out in front of him.

'You're having me on,' she said jerkily.

Not a single hint of humour—mocking or otherwise—showed in his darkly handsome, poker-faced expression. 'I am truly surprised how people's lives can alter with a blink of an eye,' he mused curiously, 'For there we both were, getting on with our independent lives with little chance of the two of us ever meeting face to face. Then I agree to do a favour for Theo and—' he glanced at the face of his solid gold wristwatch '—twenty-four hours later, almost to the minute, and here we are lovers already and planning our forthcoming marriage.'

'We are planning nothing.' Zoe drew her fingers into

her palms at her sides. 'And we already did the marriage thing last night, if you recall,' she slung back. 'I let you off the hook. Take my advice, fly away in your jet plane again and stay off the hook.'

With that she turned back to the door again.

'But I don't want to stay off the hook,' he traded, as smooth as rich cream. 'I want us to marry in haste before the tabloids get wind of it. Don't walk out of that door, Zoe,' he warned then, very seriously. 'This is far from finished just because you prefer it to be. We have other people to consider.'

'If you're talking about Theo…'

'And your brother,' he tagged on. 'Plus all the other people out there who are reliant on the Kanellis and Pallis business empires remaining healthy and strong.'

Now he was injecting something new into this discussion that trickled a slither of ice down Zoe's back. 'What other people?' she questioned warily.

'Our shareholders,' he provided. 'Our subsidiary companies that rely on us for their business, and the thousands of individuals we employ between us across the globe. With Theo living in seclusion on his island, I have been the face of both companies for the last two years. I drive them, I keep them stable and strong.

She was listening even though she still faced the door, Anton noted grimly. Zoe Kanellis might want to hate everything her Greek grandfather represented, but she couldn't bring herself to ignore what he was saying to her about everyone else involved.

'During my two-year reign, it has been taken as a given that I would inherit from Theo one day, therefore it went without needing to be said that I must have a vested interest in maintaining his business fortunes. Then your story broke and both Pallis and Kanellis stock did a swan-dive into the pits of alarm. Panic hit the volatile stock markets. They feared the appearance of Theo's relatives was about to put me out in the cold.'

'And has it?' The question was jerked from her but she still did not turn round to look at him.

'That is for Theo to decide.' Anton shrugged off that side of this discussion because it wasn't important right now. 'The thing is, Zoe, when that article and its photographs appeared this morning our stock-price shot back up the market rankings like it had been rocket-propelled. Everyone loves a good, solid merger, and what could be more solid than a merger of marriage between you and I?'

Altering his stance, and his mood, Anton straightened up from the desk and began walking towards her. She looked like a trapped bird hovering helplessly in front of a solid object, he observed, holding on to his grim intent that he was not about to let her fly away from this. He laid his hands on her shoulders and felt her quiver and stiffen as he turned her around. That she did not shrug him off, though, told him that her natural intelligence had already started to scan the wider picture he had just mapped out. Without either of them saying a word, he guided her back to the chair by the desk and invited her to sit down again.

'So this is about business.' Tossing her head, Zoe refused to sit. If they were negotiating terms then she preferred to stand while they thrashed it out. 'I have become a Kanellis asset that you need to use to keep both companies flying up there in the stratosphere?'

'It affects me too, *agape mou*.'

'Don't call me that.' Who did he think he was? 'I am not your *darling* and I have no wish to be.'

'And to think I used to believe myself to be quite a catch.'

Ignoring his attempt at sardonic self-mockery, she said,

'I still don't see why I need to be involved in this in any way. All you have to do is get Theo to announce you as his heir and the rest will take care of itself.'

'But Theo won't announce me as his heir because I am not. You and your brother are.'

Stunned by that claim, Zoe stared at him. 'We can't be. He didn't know we even existed until three weeks ago! And I don't *want* to be his heir to anything and neither does Toby!'

'You're sure about that?' Resting back against the desk again, Anton held her sparkling, defiant gaze. 'I think you are failing your brother if you make that kind of decision for him before he is old enough to decide for himself.

'And the thing is, Zoe,' he speared home grimly, 'Whether you want it or not, you are now responsible for the good health and wellbeing of the Kanellis name and all that responsibility entails. So you had better think fast about what you want do about it, because if it ever gets out there that you want nothing to do with your grandfather then the rocket ship will crash and burn—make no mistake about it—and it will probably take me down with it as it goes.'

'People aren't that stupid as to crush two companies on my say so,' Zoe protested, frowning as she did, though, because she wasn't absolutely sure about it.

'The stock market is all about risk and intuition. They do not like uncertainty. Theo's health is failing. Everybody knows this, though we try our best to keep speculation down to rumour rather than hard fact. While no one thought to question my place in his life, everything ran along smoothly. Now the market is reacting like a heart-attack victim, peaking up then shooting down depending on what snippet of information leaks out. A marriage between you and me would calm the problem.'

The grim picture he was painting her was so frighteningly bleak, Zoe gave in and lowered herself into the chair. She might want to feel nothing about any of this but it wasn't quite working out like that. She did not follow the stock markets—why would she? She'd never had more than a spare fifty pounds to spend at any one time in her entire life. Until recently, her only concern about money had been the growing size of her student loan and how she was ever going to pay it off. However, she would have had to be living on another planet not to have heard all about the unstable nature of the world's stock markets ever since the big crash.

Were they really still so sensitive that they could rip two global businesses apart on mere speculation and rumour, or be soothed by a simple thing like a marriage between Anton and herself?

The trammelling pressure of uncertainty held her silent as she stared down at her hands twisted together on her lap. She thought about her father next, and her fierce sense of loyalty to him. Would he have wanted her to do this thing? Her instincts said no. Her instincts reminded her of the countless times she had watched him arrive home from work looking ready to drop on his feet. He'd worked two jobs to earn them a decent living, his week days filled with the grease and grime as a car mechanic, his weekends filled with waiting on tables at a local restaurant. Yet not once had she heard him even whisper the seed of an idea that he wanted to return to his old life here in Greece.

And how many nights had he stretched out on the sofa in front of the TV and barely move again until it was time for bed? How many weekends had her mother spent quietly on her own while her husband had served other people with a smile he probably forced onto his tired face? *And how many years had Theo Kanellis spent being waited on by men like my dad?* she tagged on bitterly. The private islands, the yachts, the planes…

'Your father's death hit Theo very hard,' Anton inserted quietly, choosing his next words with care. 'He has weeks not months to live, Zoe. Try to dig deep inside yourself and see if you really want a fading old man tormented by regrets watch his empire fall into tatters while the life fades from him.'

'Now that,' she whispered thickly, 'Was emotional blackmail.'

A white handkerchief arrived on her lap. 'It is a very emotional time.'

'There's not much emotional input in a marriage of convenience,' she said, picking up the handkerchief and using it to dab the corners of her eyes. 'But, as the article said, business is business after all.'

Anton took a few moments to rerun that last remark a couple of times before he spoke again. 'Is that a yes?' he asked for confirmation. 'You will marry me?'

Well, it wasn't a no, Zoe thought with a sniff. 'You're going to appear a real money-grabbing monster.'

'I am Greek,' he countered. 'We make business deals of this nature all the time.'

Did she detect a note of rueful satire in his voice just then? Glancing up at him, she saw he just looked relaxed as if they'd been chatting about the weather. When had he suddenly become indifferent to being labelled a gold-digger?

'Of course, I will attempt to redeem my character,' he murmured thoughtfully then. 'I will have it put about that I leaked the information about who your father was, in an effort to bring the family feud to an end.'

'No way will you do that!' Zoe shot back to her feet. 'Don't you *dare* bring my father into this!'

'Because he deserved to be recognised as Theo's son,'

he continued as if she hadn't interrupted. 'I will let it be known that I feel guilty that I had not brought the situation to a head a lot sooner, then maybe father and son could have had a chance to reconcile before—'

'But you didn't know before!' Zoe jumped in quickly before he could finish what he had been about to say. She didn't want to hear it. She *never* wanted to hear that word in relation to either of her parents. She even shut her eyes tightly in an effort to shut the whole painfully wretched thought out of her head.

'You cannot know that for certain.' He was relentless in the face of her obvious distress. 'Nobody knows what I knew about Leander Kanellis before—the accident,' he changed the last part when she sucked in a painful breath.

No, Zoe accepted, she didn't know that. While he had been playing Theo's adopted son, he could easily have been keeping a covert eye on Theo's real son and family, just in case they became a problem for him.

He could read her like an open book, Anton observed grimly. She was now seeing him as the heartlessly manipulating, lying cheat with the seduction of Theo's granddaughter in mind long before the two of them had even met up.

'It may be a good idea if we agree that you and I met months ago—somewhere away from London. We will fill in the details later,' he persisted, nailing her to the rug beneath her feet with the depths to which she now perceived he was willing to deceive. 'It will be a classic case of love at first sight. When we discovered we were—otherwise connected—things became complicated.'

'So you decided to shoot off to New York to indulge in an affair with your modelling friend?'

Anton pulled a face at the quick sarcastic putdown. She might be down, but her brain was still functioning OK.

'We had a trial separation.' He covered that problem. 'You were very busy with your university studies, and concerned how your father was going to react to our—romance. So we decided to go our separate ways for a time to see if what we felt for each other was just—'

'Lust, not Romeo and Juliet.'

He dared to send her a grin that plucked at Zoe's heart strings for some unfathomable reason. 'You are catching on.'

Folding her arms across her front to crush the sensation, Zoe faced him squarely. 'So let me see if I can have this right. You are the— How old are you?' she paused to ask.

'Thirty-one,' he provided.

Zoe nodded. 'So, you are the thirty-one-year-old lovelorn tycoon who flies off to find solace in another woman's bed, while I remain the untouched virgin waiting for you to come back to me and claim your—gift?'

'It was a fabulous gift, *agape mou*,' he murmured softly. 'I will treasure it for the rest of our lives.'

'Don't overstretch your ability to hold to a promise,' snapped Zoe. 'We both know you're lousy at keeping them.'

'I will keep this one.' Suddenly he was deadly serious. 'Bring to our marriage bed the passionate woman I met last night and I will endeavour to keep her happy and content.'

He was talking sex. A light bulb of alarm lit up in Zoe's head. 'We are not going to share a bed! Where the heck do you get the nerve to turn a cold business-arrangement into a promise of good sex?'

'Easy, I have been thinking of little else since you walked in here.'

The dark and husky admission sent Zoe backing off a couple of steps in an attempt to distance herself from what he had said. Why hadn't she noticed before that the whole room was loaded with sexual tension? she asked herself suddenly, noticing it now and feeling it in the new rush of awareness that swept down her front.

'Ours will be a full and fruitful marriage, *kardia mou*, not an empty showcase filled with coldness,' he continued in the same husky tone. 'How else does it have a chance at success?'

He was talking long-term here. Zoe blinked slowly then gave an adamantly negative shake of her head. 'This will be a temporary arrangement lasting only until—until this current crisis with the stock markets goes away.'

'You think?'

'I know.' She was staring into his eyes again—a dangerous thing to do, especially when that glow took them over, the one that set her heart racing when he slowly straightened up from the desk.

Too late, she realised that she'd just challenged his sexual ego. That the sun flowing against the side of his face as he moved was adding a worryingly hypnotic effect to his eyes. She couldn't look away from them, couldn't halt the tingling tremor which hit the tips of her now aching breasts and that other place low down between her thighs.

'S-stay back,' she stammered when he took a step in her direction.

'Why?' With devastating simplicity he pinned her to the spot with the question when she knew she should be running for her life. 'You want me. Do you think I cannot read your body language? You have been wishing I would strip my clothes off since you walked in here. In fact, if I did start stripping, you would probably rush to help.'

'Isn't that just typically arrogant of you to think that?' Zoe heaved in a deep breath while managing to take another couple of steps backwards. 'Just—just because you were my first lover does not make me suddenly obsessed with s-sex!'

'Your pupils have dilated; your cheeks are wearing a very informative soft pink glow.' Reaching out with a hand, he touched one of her cheeks with a fingertip. Zoe pulled back her head so sharply she hurt the muscles in the back of her neck. 'And you are trembling,' he observed as he took another step closer. 'I can hear the husk of arousal in your breathless voice. And the most intriguing thing is that you are still such a stranger to your own feelings you don't even recognise the signals you're giving off.'

Her cheeks had fired into flames now. Anxiously she continued to back off. *He likes stalking you like a predator,* a little voice inside her head warned her. *Stay still, hold your ground, outface him.*

She pulled to a stop. 'Well, there speaks the man of experience,' she traded bitterly. 'But what else can I expect of a man who's been sleeping around since he knew there was a difference between male and female?'

'You expected a thirty-one-year-old virgin in your bed?' He actually sounded incredulous.

'Yes!' Zoe flung at him hotly, 'Why not? My mother was my father's first lover! She was his! They spent twenty-three years together and never wanted or took other lovers! They were both very proud of that!'

'Oh, what it's like to live with perfection,' he mocked derisively. 'Did they fill your head with the same ideals, Zoe? Are you waiting for your perfect virgin lover to come along and sweep you into lifelong married bliss?'

Her cheeks burned all the hotter. 'Well, I won't find him in you, will I?'

His dark head went back. 'Definitely not. You will find a well-rounded, very experienced man who has played the field long enough to be ready to give you his complete loyalty and the pleasure of his sexual experience.'

'*If* I decide to have you, that is!'

His eyes narrowed. He'd walked out of the sunlight now so all she saw was the dark glow of yet more predator challenge framed by eyelashes as black as night.

'Oh, you will have me,' he told her softly. 'Do you know why you will have me?'

'If you don't s-stop all of this I will…'

The gap between them suddenly closed like a door being slammed shut on her resistance. Zoe could feel herself giving in to him even as he started to lower his dark head.

'No—please don't.' She uttered this one final stab at resistance but she stared at the sensual shape of his mouth as she said it.

'Liar,' he whispered, then teased her with the gentlest touch of his tongue to the corner of her mouth. When she shivered, he laughed softly and did it again. 'Think about how it will feel to get naked with me,' he urged. 'Think about acquiring exclusive rights on all of this…'

'This' was his hands taking hold of her hips and drawing her against him. 'This' was the evidence of his desire for her pressing against her and liquidising the bones in her legs. He settled light, moist kisses across her lower lip, coaxing it to part from its upper partner. When she refused to let it, he raised his head up a little, just enough to scan whatever was happening in her eyes. What he saw written there made him smile. Then he took her. He took her by storm and with lethal precision, covering both of her lips and prising them apart with a heated delving of absolute possession that rendered her helpless, because desire was swimming up inside her like a tidal wave.

It wasn't fair. Zoe whimpered out a strangled protest just before all the defensive tension locking her muscles snapped. On a low, anguished groan she slid her clenched fists up over his shoulders, stretched out her fingers, curled them into the firm flesh of his nape then moulded herself up against his hardness and heat. Her surrender was rewarded by the fire of his passion. He kissed her so deeply she lost touch with everything but the river of pleasure pouring through her blood. Every nerve-ending came alive with a sexual sparkle that dizzied her brain and made her cling to him all the more. The flat of his hand laid claim to the base of her spine to hold her tight to the power of his muscular frame.

Inside she melted like butter. By the time he let them both up for air again, she was a quivering mess of shell-shocked heat. His tie had gone awry and the buttons on his shirt had been wrenched open—by her; it must have been her that did it—exposing the breadth of his chest with whorls of black hair and sexily ridged muscles. And he was breathing fast. It was her one—her only—consolation to stand here in his arms and watch his chest move swiftly as he fought for breath.

'Do yourself a favour,' he ground out harshly. 'And rethink your role as my wife.'

With that he stepped away from her. It was so ruthless a separation it left Zoe swaying where she stood. Then he swung his back to her and began to fasten up his shirt. A blinding kind of sensual confusion throbbed like an extra heart inside her chest, and even that came with a taunt because her breasts were so heavy and so tight they visibly palpitated against her white vest-top.

She felt she had only one course of action left open to her. She turned and walked as straight as she could, through the door and out of it without even trying to utter a single word.

Caught, tried and hung by her own body's weakness,

Zoe thought numbly as she paced her bedroom floor like someone trapped. How had it happened? How had they gone from complete strangers and hostile enemies to hot, greedy, passionate, insatiable lovers in the space of twenty-four hours?

'I don't see why you're making me do this,' Zoe complained tautly as the helicopter they were travelling in sped across the crystal-blue waters of the Aegean. 'Couldn't it have waited until I was ready for it? Af-after the wedding, maybe, or…?'

'The world watches us, *agape mou*,' Anton responded evenly, reminding her of that glass case he had mentioned just over a week ago when somehow—she still could not work out why she had done it—she had agreed to marry him.

'What is there for them to see? I've been hiding away on your island all week while you do whatever it is you do each day when you leave.'

'I work. It is expected of a power-mad, gold-digging empire builder.'

Zoe grimaced at his quotation from one of the more imaginative tabloids.

'And Theo wants to see you,' he added. 'It was either bring you to him or watch him carry out his threat and come to see you. I could not risk that he might be bluffing,' he explained, frowning. 'The flight probably would have killed him.'

Toby let out a squeak in demand for attention then. He did not like the helicopter ride. He'd sobbed his heart out from the moment they'd taken off until Zoe couldn't stand it, and had released him from his seat so she could pick him up and cuddle him. When he still would not calm down, Anton had plucked the baby out of her arms to try soothing him himself, and it still annoyed Zoe that it had worked. The moment Toby had felt Anton's strong arms go around him, he had just shut up, as if he'd sensed safety and calmness there instead of the anxiety and tension Zoe had been giving off.

But then the baby and the man had become good friends over the last week. Whereas she and Anton had become—lovers. Proper lovers. Lovers who slept in the same bed.

The first night he had come to her. He'd slid between her sheets, ignored her furious protests, drawn her towards him and had taken up where he'd left off after her humiliating downfall in his study.

The second night he'd come to her room, dragged her out of bed and trailed her, protesting, along the landing into his room and bed. That was the same day the new nanny had flown in. Her name was Melissa Stefani; she spoke both Greek and English, and most irritating of all she was nice. Martha went back to her full-time studies. Melissa was currently occupying the seat up front next to their pilot.

Zoe had eaten, lived and slept with Anton as if they were already a married couple. And his bedroom door was firmly closed each night so she wouldn't hear her brother when he woke up. That she knew she'd started to look less drawn around the edges, did not sweeten Zoe's present mood at all.

Also, during the last week, she had been treated to a taste of what it was going to be like being Anton Pallis's wife in a thousand little ways, like the way Anthea now deferred to her every decision about the general running of the household—as if she had a clue how to run a house that big.

She'd been expected to decide what they ate for dinner, and if they had flowers on the table, or candles, or both.

When she would have preferred to curl up with a book somewhere quiet, she'd been treated to tours of linen closets and the long row of glass-fronted cabinets displaying extensive china dinner-services most of which, she had been proudly informed, were priceless. She knew nothing about art. It wasn't her bag. But the walls were full of it. Even the huge, ornate mirrors hanging on the walls were apparently priceless antiques with lustrous histories attached to each one.

So what had she learnt? That Anton's ancestors had been respected collectors of all that was beautiful. But she could not tell the difference between a Claude Monet and an Édouard Manet. However, what really struck her very hard was that her car-mechanic father probably had.

And now here she was, taking her first trip off the island since she'd arrived on it. And it was a trip to visit her grandfather, who probably had his home filled with the same status symbols of wealth and good taste.

'I hope he's not expecting all smiles and forgiveness from me,' she sniped, so sharply on the defensive it was like she was sitting on pins.

'I would think it would require a miracle for you to want to give Theo your understanding and sympathy.'

She had grown used to this form of passive sarcasm from Anton over the last week, but what she refused to get used to was being spoken to as if she was a sulky child.

'We can always call the wedding off, if you're having second thoughts?' she offered coolly.

She heard him draw in an audible breath which brought her head around to look at him. He was lounging in his seat with Toby resting against his shoulder. For once he wasn't wearing one of his million-dollar suits, though the faded jeans and a grey polo-shirt he had on beneath a linen jacket screamed stylish sophistication at her… Oh God, she thought restlessly, he looked gorgeous.

'Was that a trick question?' he posed curiously.

A sullen shrug of a narrow shoulder and Zoe decided she wished she hadn't said it. She went to turn her head away again, only Anton wasn't going to let her off the hook that easily. His hand arrived on her arm, applying just enough pressure to make her aware of his strength.

'Don't talk down to me like I'm your kid sister, OK?' She launched at him while seething inside for reasons really quite divorced from this particular complaint she was using as a vent. 'There might be a huge gap of nine long years between my age and yours, and a whole lot of obnoxious arrogance, but unless you have a thing about bossing around minors treat with respect my *adult* right to an opinion or I *will* call off the wedding!'

She tugged her arm free, refusing to wince when it hurt as she did. Yet another silence clattered down around them. Zoe glared at the back of Melissa's head and hoped to goodness the nanny and the pilot had not heard what she'd said. She didn't even know what was the matter with her, yet on another level she did know very well that all this restless, bad-tempered tension was because she was at war with herself rather than with him. How had she allowed herself to become his puppet? How had he managed to seduce her so thoroughly that she'd stopped being herself? She looked at him and she wanted him—*wanted.* Every time. Even when she hated him.

'Zoe…'

'Shut up,' she breathed tautly.

Right now she felt like a pubescent teenager, so switched on to her emotions they were swirling inside her like an unruly mob. They trampled over her self-control and her ability to think with her normal, calm logic. They choked her up and drove her to do and say things she would never normally have done or said.

'We are here,' Anton murmured.

Fluttering her glance sideways, a different set of emotions surged up and attacked her. For down there below them, rising up out of the glistening blue sea, was the tiny horseshoe-shaped island of her father's birth.

CHAPTER TEN

HURRYING clear of the helicopter's rotor blades, Zoe paused to look around her new surroundings. They'd landed on a stretch of grass spread between a pretty crescent-shaped beach and a surprisingly modest-looking single-storey house with bright white walls and a wooden veranda shaded from the sun by the slope of the roof.

Arriving at her side with Toby still curled into his shoulder, Anton followed the track of her gaze. 'Theo does not like change,' he told her quietly. 'The original house—the middle part you can see is different from the two outer wings—belonged to his fisherman grandfather who built it himself. When Theo bought the island he changed nothing until he married your grandmother. It was she who insisted the house be extended to accommodate her love of throwing parties here. When she died, Theo stopped coming here for years and the house more or less stagnated. He preferred to use his house in Glyfada on the mainland. He said it was more convenient for his offices in Athens and the airport, but I think he just hated coming here because he missed her so much.'

'Kassandra.' Zoe murmured the name of her paternal grandmother.

'The same as your middle name,' Anton confirmed.

And one of the very few marks of recognition her father had made of his Greek roots. 'Did—did you ever meet her?'

'She died before I came here. Shall we go up to the house?'

If that was his polite way of telling her this was not the time for this kind of conversation, it succeeded in shutting her up. Anyway, she was too nervous to hold on to a particular thought for more than two seconds before her attention returned to the house and, more particularly, who was waiting inside it to meet his grandson.

Anton was feeling no less tense about this meeting. He had fought with Theo against it until the stubborn old man had threatened to fly over to Thalia and gatecrash what he'd called, 'Anton's damned arrogant hijacking of his plans.'

Kidnapper, hijacker... His sins were piling up.

Melissa was waiting for them beneath the shade of the veranda. As they reached the steps which led up onto the wooden decking, the front door opened and an elderly woman dressed all in black stepped out. She shot a curious glance over Zoe and Melissa then turned the look at the small baby he held in his arms.

'So you bring him at last,' she announced like a reprimand, then took an eager step forward as if to grab the baby right out of his arms. Alarm went tumbling through Zoe; impulsively she made a move to halt the old woman but Anton got in first.

'Behave, Dorothea,' he censured mildly. 'This is not the moment for snatching babies from their loved ones.'

Flushing a little, the old woman drew back again, then turned around and walked back into the house. They followed, Anton standing back to allow Zoe and Melissa to precede him into a surprisingly large square-shaped hallway which must have been the main room of the original house.

'You had better go in before he blows a fuse. He is in there.' Dorothea waved a hand at a door leading off to the left of them. 'I will bring coffee.'

'After you have shown Miss Stefani somewhere she can sit and be comfortable while she is not needed,' Anton countered evenly.

He was pulling rank on the housekeeper and it did not need special powers to recognise that the two of them sparred like this as the norm. The old woman flashed him a look then gave a huff and walked off, with poor Melissa reluctantly trailing behind.

'Dorothea has worked for Theo for so long she sometimes forgets her role in his house. She is harmless, however, if stood up to.'

Great, thought Zoe. So Dorothea was just another person she had to stand up to. That made two of them, and that was before she even got to meet Theo Kanellis.

Stepping up to the door the housekeeper had indicated, Anton waited for Zoe to catch him up. She watched him run his eyes over her as she walked towards him and knew he would see the nervous tension in control of her body inside the apricot dress she was wearing.

'OK?' he asked softly when she stopped beside him.

I wish, thought Zoe, taking a moment to breathe in and out a couple of times before she turned to him and lifted her arms up. 'I will take Toby now.'

She felt him wanting to say something, felt his hesitation inch her stress levels up another whole notch. Perhaps he knew how she was feeling because he released a small sigh then lifted the sleeping boy from his shoulder and transferred him into her care. Toby uttered a quivery sigh and curled in against her as he usually did, and Zoe lifted up her chin then turned to face the door.

'Taking him on, *agape mou*?'

You bet, Zoe thought. 'I am ready for what's coming next if that is that you're asking me,' she returned, then tensed up her spine when he reached out to gently ease a trapped lock of her hair out from beneath her brother's resting cheek.

'I won't let him eat you,' he promised.

Pressing her lips together, Zoe nodded her head.

On another small sigh—because it must be obvious to him that she was trying her best to shut him out right now—Anton reached for the handle and pushed the door open. She found herself staring down the length of the large, bright airy room with the sunlight softened by the creamy blinds lowered across the windows.

She saw him then and her heart gave a heavy thump against her ribs. He was standing in front of a thick stone fireplace, and that shocked her, because sickly and fading Theo Kanellis was not. He stood tall and proud, emitting a kind of inner strength that rolled into her, even if he was standing there leaning heavily on the walking stick he held clamped close to one long elegantly suited leg.

It was like looking at her father. Or how her father would have looked if he'd had the chance to reach his seventh decade, she amended, feeling that low ache of grief she carried around with her make itself felt. He was the same height and had the same-shaped eyes as her father, the same rapier-thin nose and striking bone structure—though there was no resemblance in this man's head of thick silver hair or the unsmiling mouth.

He was staring at her with a fierce and fixed intensity that warned her he was not about to cower if she turned the hostility on. 'Well, don't just stand there as if you want to turn around again and run,' he bit out.

The deep rasp of his voice made Toby jerk against her shoulder. As she soothed her brother with the stroke of her hand, the light touch of Anton's fingertips came to rest low on her back as if in reassurance, and the nerve endings there tingled in response.

She was glad he was here. At this precise moment while she was a mixed-up mess of conflicting feelings about this meeting; it was comforting to feel his presence like a protective wall at her back. When those fingertips urged her forward, she moved on legs that felt as if they had turned to sponge.

Theo Kanellis watched her every step. He took in her hair flowing free around her shoulders, the simple cut of her apricot dress and the long, slender length of her legs. When she pulled to a halt four feet away from him, he flicked his gaze up to take in the electric-blue steadiness of her gaze. They continued to stare at each other for what felt like minutes, facing off like wary adversaries waiting to see which one of them broke first.

It would not be her, Zoe told herself. She was determined to keep silent until he said something worthy of an answer.

It came. 'You look like your mother,' he growled, his mouth turning downwards as if in contempt.

'Thank you,' Zoe replied smoothly.

'And very English,' he added like a prod in the chest.

'I am very English,' she confirmed with studied composure.

Curiously, he still had not looked at Toby. In fact the next person he turned his fierce gaze upon was Anton. 'I suppose you think you've pulled off a great coup.'

'Depends on the coup you are referring to,' the man

standing tall and steady as a rock behind her responded. 'How are you, Theo?'

At last, someone had tried to inject some normal manners into the proceedings. Not that it was a hit with Theo Kanellis. 'You can cut out that rubbish,' he snapped, then lifted up the hand clenched around his walking stick. 'Sit down over there, where I can see you,' he instructed Zoe, waving the stick at one of two wing-backed chairs standing either side of the fireplace. 'You,' he said to Anton, 'Can make yourself scarce.'

'I will leave when your granddaughter indicates to me that she wants me to leave,' Anton came back smooth as silk to her grandfather's grating rasp.

It was like the clash of the Titans, thought Zoe, every one of her senses alert to the fact that she was in the presence of two very powerful male personalities here. Theo Kanellis continued to glare at Anton while he maintained his solid stance behind her with his fingers still in contact with her back.

Yet there was something about the older man's demeanour—Zoe wasn't sure what it was—that made her decide to break the pulsing deadlock between the two men. Moving over to the chair her grandfather had pointed at, she lowered herself down on its edge, which freed Anton from his protective stance without her needing to say anything.

Because she did not want him to go. It came as a small shock to realise how reliant she felt on his presence right now. What he did was to wait until Theo Kanellis had lowered himself into the other chair, then he walked across the room to stand by the window as if he was taking the middle path by staying in the room while withdrawing to the edges of the fray.

'So, you had better let me have a look at him.' Theo Kanellis fired his first look at Toby.

Experiencing a stab of over-protectiveness for her brother which made her want to hug him all the closer to her front, she forced down the impulse, lifted the baby off her shoulder and brought him to rest in the cradle of her arms, then twisted slightly on the chair so his grandfather could see his tiny sleeping face.

Tension plucked at the silence again while grandfather stared at grandson. Zoe couldn't tell if he was impressed or unimpressed by what he saw, but the growl in his voice thickened slightly when he looked back at her and said, 'At least he looks Greek.'

She had no argument with that observation. Her brother did look very Greek. 'Yes,' she agreed.

'Tobias…' he growled next. 'What kind of name is that for a Greek boy?'

'It is the name my parents chose for Toby before they…'

Zoe let her voice trail to a muffled standstill when she realised what she had almost said. Lowering her eyes from the ones watching her so intently, she swallowed tautly and just hoped that the sudden pang of grief she'd suffered had not showed on her face.

But her grandfather had seen it. He shifted restlessly where he sat. 'I am—sorry for your loss,' he murmured uncomfortably. 'It is unfortunate that we should meet for the first time under such—tragic circumstances.'

Unable to find a single thing to say in response to this offer of sympathy, from the man who had cut his own son out of his life twenty three years ago, all Zoe could do was nod.

Anton had told her that her grandfather had regrets about the past and she could feel those regrets pulsing in the space between them right now. Was it wrong of her to feel bitter about that? Because she did feel bitter, and angry on her father's behalf; hurt for her mother who had lived those same twenty-three years knowing she was not an acceptable wife for this man's son. And, yes, she was hurt on her own behalf that she too had not been worthy of his notice.

'OK,' growled that rasping voice. 'I can see that you don't want to talk about my son, so we will get down to business instead. Anton tells me you are prepared to marry him to help stop your inheritance from going down the drain with my stock.'

Zoe lifted her chin to look at him, 'I have no interest in your money,' she informed him.

'So you are agreeing to throw your life away on this ruthless devil out of the kindness of your heart?'

'No.' She felt the heat of temper attempting to flood her cheeks at his assessment of what she was doing as mercenary. 'I'm doing it for my brother and his future.'

'You mean you fell into bed with him and, like a lot of females before you, could not bear the idea of having to crawl out of it again?'

The remark was scathing enough to make her lose control over the blush. It did not help that he was more or less telling it exactly how it was. She had fallen into bed with Anton—*dragged him* there in her own wretched eagerness. 'I am not answerable to you for anything I do, Mr Kanellis,' she said icily. 'So you might as well stop—'

'Mr Kanellis, heh?' he interrupted then let out a short laugh. 'And not answerable to me… Well, let us just try testing that, missy. For here is my counter offer: marry Anton, and neither you nor your brother will get a single penny from me. Drop Anton and come here to live with me, and I will leave the lot to you and your brother when I die.'

Zoe stared at this man she was supposed to call her grandfather. There was fire in his eyes, shot through with unholy amusement because he believed he had thrown her into a loop. Somewhere on the periphery of her vision she was aware that Anton stood like a dark silhouette against the light of the slatted window. He continued to remain silent as if he too was waiting to hear how she was going to respond to this challenge her grandfather had thrown down at her feet.

'Think about it,' Theo Kanellis urged. 'Think about the power I am offering you to avenge the man I put in your father's place. You can cut him out of this with a simple yes to my offer and scupper his plans for revenge on what Leander did to—'

'That's enough.' Anton suddenly stepped forward, his voice sounding hard, like the crack of a whip. 'We are supposed to be trying to mend fences here, Theo, not draging the ugliness of the past up again.'

'But—what is he talking about?' Twisting round on the chair; Zoe looked up at Anton, whose hard profile was fiercely clenched.

'He is talking about nothing,' he clipped out. 'Your grandfather is just testing you while trying to make mischief for me at the same time.'

'But…' Zoe stopped to moisten her trembling lips, her mind spinning backwards to the actual words Theo Kanellis had said. 'He m-mentioned revenge. Why would he say that unless—?'

'Gomoto!' the older man burst out in surprise. 'She does not know, does she?'

He went off into sudden great roars of laughter. Toby woke up with a start and began sobbing like mad. At the exact same moment the baby started crying, her grandfather stopped laughing and started coughing, the sound scored by violent wheezes as he struggled for air and sent Anton striding over to him squat down at his feet.

'Now look what you've done, you crazy old fool,' he muttered with an odd kind of roughness as he closed a hand over one of the older man's shoulders while reaching from something dangling over the arm of the chair.

It was a panic button. Recognising it instantly, Zoe shot to her feet. She was trying desperately to soothe the wailing baby while she watched in growing horror her grandfather fight to squeeze air into his congested lungs.

Then everything turned dizzyingly chaotic when the door flew open to allow a young man to rush in. He had the intent look and the manner of a nurse the way he strode down the room and bent over Theo Kanellis, almost knocking Anton out of his way in the process. Both men went in a huddle over Theo. Toby kept on crying. Dorothea appeared, puffing and panting, with an anxious-looking Melissa hurrying in her wake.

Standing up, Anton threw the nanny a glance. 'Take Toby away from here and calm him,' he instructed. Without quite knowing how it all happened, Zoe found herself relieved of her brother, Anton was hustling her out of the room. She caught a glimpse of Melissa disappearing towards the back of the house and she could hear Dorothea scolding Theo. Then Anton pulled the door firmly shut behind them, and was trailing across the hall with one of his hands clamped around her hand while his other hand threw open a door.

It led to a study with heavy dark furniture. Anton pushed her down onto a big red-velvet sofa. 'Wh-what just happened to him?' she whispered, still so shaken up she couldn't stop trembling.

'You thought that his health had taken a sudden upturn due to you agreeing to come here?'

Sardonic though he sounded, Zoe could see from the

angles in his face that he had been no less affected by what had just taken place.

'I hadn't got as far as thinking anything about the state of his health except that he looked so—strong.' She swallowed the last word on a blameworthy gulp, for she'd been so involved in protecting her own line of defence she had not thought to question her grandfather's show of strength until it had collapsed.

'Which is exactly how he wanted you to see him.' Turning away to walk across the room, Anton opened what turned out to be a drinks cabinet. 'He is a stubborn old fool who wanted to meet you standing on his own two feet. You just witnessed the result of his damn stupid folly.'

Pouring a splash of brandy into two glasses, Anton turned and walked back to sit down beside her and handed her a glass. 'Drink it,' he instructed when all she did was stare blindly down into the glass.

Zoe shook her head. 'And—and the other stuff?' she asked. 'The revenge thing that started him laughing like that in the first place?'

Anton knocked his brandy back like a veteran. 'He was trying to wind us both up. There are so few occasions when he gets the opportunity to exercise his razor-edged cunning these days, seemingly he could not miss this chance.'

But that wasn't the only reason. Zoe could see he was pale beneath his tan and there were score lines of tension grooving his mouth. 'Don't fob me off with more lies, Anton,' she said on a seething breath of impatience. 'He thought it hilarious that I did not know something he clearly expected me to know. I want to know what that something is!'

Throwing himself back against the sofa cushions, Anton let out a sigh and closed his eyes. He should have seen this coming. Why had he not seen it coming? He had known within ten minutes of meeting her that she had no idea why Theo and his son had never attempted to mend the rift between them. Zoe believed that Theo was the unforgiving despot who'd cut his son out of his life because Leander had dared to humiliate him by jilting the bride Theo had picked out for him.

He wished it could have been that simple. He wished even more that he had not let his normal common sense take a hike in favour of lusting after Theo's granddaughter to the point that he'd convinced himself everything was going to turn out just fine in the end.

Take her to bed. Enjoy her. Put the marriage deal on the table. Appeal to her sympathetic side to get her to agree. Bed her again, over and over, then make this magnanimous gesture by bringing her here to heal the family rift before you take her as your wife. Theo was supposed to be virtually on his death bed. He was supposed to play his role as deeply regretful father struggling with guilt because his son had died before he'd had a chance to try and put things right.

'You *are* in this for the money, aren't you?' Zoe fired at him tautly.

Anton winced as the accusation cut him deep. 'No,' he denied. 'I don't need Theo's money. I have plenty enough of my own.'

'Well, open your eyes and look at me while you repeat that!' Slamming her untouched glass down, Zoe lurched to her feet on a quiver of trembling limbs.

He did it. He lifted up his heavy eyelids and looked at her. Zoe tensed up on a protesting gasp. 'How *dare* you look at me in that way right now?'

Easy, thought Anton, watching her quiver with fury inside the apricot-coloured dress. One swift move on his part and he could take her away from all of this, here, right now, on Theo's couch. It was a much more tempting prospect than allowing this particular conversation to drag out to its miserable conclusion. Hot sex on the crest of a tidal wave of wild emotions; he could even taste the pleasure of it inside his mouth. And he could read from her body language that she was struggling not to let herself respond to it from the warm cheeks, the shivering heave of her breasts, the hands curled into tight fists at her sides.

She looked him in the eyes and she wanted him. It had always been like that from the start.

'Say no to your grandfather's money, *agape mou…*' Distract to divert; he knew exactly what he was doing. 'Walk away from it—with me—right now. I can promise you, you will never regret it. An hour, and we can be back home enjoying the kind of siesta that turns your beautiful bones to wax.'

'My—my grandfather is sick and you want to—' Almost choking on the words, she turned her back on him in disgust—though which of them the disgust was aimed at was a moot point, Anton mused as he watched her wrap her arms around the hammering thump of her heart.

'And Toby?' she flung back. 'You were the one who told me I should think about him instead of myself.'

'I can take care of my own,' he countered. 'Toby will want for nothing so long as he remains in my care.'

It was strange how a few supposedly reassuring words could turn her crowding senses into pin pricks of ice. She swung back around to face him. 'In your care as what—guardian of his fortune, by any chance?'

So they were back to that again. Narrowing his eyes on her challenging stance, he warned carefully, 'Don't do that. Don't turn this back into a gold-digging charge unless you're ready for a hard fight.'

Zoe flicked her hair back off her shoulders, the desire

to remain suspicious of him warring with a deeper instinct that told her he wasn't in this for the money-spinning power. 'So, if you are not in this to get control of Theo's money, tell me again why you bothered to bring us here at all,' she demanded. 'And then tell me why he accused you of wanting revenge.'

His silence held a kind of power of its own as he continued to lounge on the sofa, studying her through those narrowed, simmering sardonic eyes. She was not able to read the look, and it made the silence hang like an axe between them because nothing on earth was going to make her back down until he had answered the charge. But beneath her folded arms her stomach muscles felt quivery and tight because she needed so badly to hear him crush the life out of that word *revenge*, with some crystal-clear reasoning she had not managed to work out for herself just yet.

When he continued to say nothing, and eventually uncoiled his long body until he was on his feet, she found herself having to fight the urge to take a defensive step back. The enemy… Those two little words floated into her head and stayed there, reminding her of what she had stubbornly allowed herself to forget.

He stood there in what he considered casual clothes and looked a million dollars, the tall, tough tycoon with fabulous good looks and eye for style bred into him. There wasn't an inch of him that she could find to criticise—of a physical nature, that was. But what did she know about the real man, that inner core that never showed itself even when he trembled in her arms as they made love?

He was a stranger to her, and a ruthless one, or she would not even be here in Greece, Zoe concluded. She did not like herself right now for allowing herself to be seduced into believing he was anything else.

'Answer me, Anton,' she demanded, too worried now to bother to hide the anxious quaver in her voice.

He glanced down at the glass he was still holding, noticed it was empty and walked back to the drinks cabinet. Following him with her eyes, Zoe felt an aching clutch of pending agony begin to stir in her chest because she knew she was about to hear something that was going to rend her apart.

'I am not out for revenge on anyone.' It came out cool and flat as he splashed brandy into the bottom of the glass.

She felt for the right words. 'But there is—is a reason why you might be?'

'Yes.' He nodded.

Zoe took a moment to pull in a breath. 'And this—reason concerns my father.' This time it wasn't a question but a measured assumption. 'Why *did* Theo choose you to take my father's place all those years ago?'

There it was—the big question. The one Anton had been waiting for her to ask him from the moment the two of them had first met. Pulling a wry face at the golden liquid resting temptingly in the glass, he set it aside, schooled his expression into an impassive mask then turned around to face her again.

'Because Theo felt he owed it to me,' he answered levelly.

The way she was standing there with her arms still tensely folded and her vivid blue eyes fixed on him, showing her strain, he knew that she knew she was about to learn something that was going to crucify her perfect vision of the father she loved.

And he was the man who was going to do it. If he'd ever considered taking revenge on Leander Kanellis, then the success should taste very sweet right now.

But it did not taste sweet. It tasted like poison.

'You already know that your father ran away from an arranged marriage.' He made himself go on. 'What you do not seem to know is that the woman he left standing at the church altar was my recently widowed mother.'

CHAPTER ELEVEN

'YOUR...mother?' He'd said it so calmly Zoe almost missed the horrendous impact of the words themselves.

'It was supposed to be the great business-merger of two formidable families,' he said with a brief, grim smile. 'Theo wanted to merge his company with my grandfather's company. My grandfather drove a hard bargain, insisting the only way they would merge was if their two children married to cement the deal.'

It sounded so coldly calculating; Zoe shivered. 'But my father was only eighteen years old,' she said. 'How old was your mother?'

'Thirty-two—not that the ages of either of them mattered.' He grimaced. 'My mother had grown up doing as her father told her. She strove all of her life to make him proud.'

'She gave him a grandson. In Greek terms, that should have made him very proud.'

'Defending my place in this sorry tale, *agape mou*?' Anton murmured dryly. 'You surprise me.'

'I was thinking of your poor mother, not you,' Zoe countered. 'You said she'd been recently widowed. Did she love your father?'

'"Love" is not a word I would use to describe their relationship, though I was perhaps too young to understand it. I recall frost and fights and long empty spaces in which we never saw him.' He gave an idle shrug. 'My grandfather ruled our home, not my father. My father changed *his* name to Pallis as part of the deal when he married my mother. The wonders of vast wealth,' he tagged on cynically.

'And my father?' Zoe ventured. 'Was he ruled by his father?'

'Most people would have believed so until Leander disappeared on his way to the church. He surprised everyone when he did that,' Anton recalled whimsically. 'In fact, the shock was so great it gave my grandfather a heart attack which killed him. My mother shut herself away in a convent and eventually died there a few months later of humiliation and shame.

'While she was doing that,' he continued in the same shatteringly calm way, 'Your grandmother, on her way to England to beg her son to come back home and do his duty to his family, was killed when the helicopter she was travelling in crashed into the Aegean—Theo lost the only woman he had ever loved.'

Edging carefully backwards, Zoe lowered herself down on the sofa before her trembling legs gave away. Her grandmother; dear God. 'I can see now why Theo never forgave him,' she murmured across the fragile edge of her breath.

But even more painful was the realisation that her father had been living for all those years since with the heavy burden of guilt for his own mother's death.

Leander had never managed to forgive himself.

Suddenly it all began to make such a terribly sad kind of sense: her father's refusal to talk about his Greek family, the way his eyes would cloud over whenever Greece was mentioned on the TV. Even her mother, her quiet, gentle mother, must have known that their marriage had been built on the worst of foundations—guilt and grief.

'Theo was left alone, deeply embittered,' Anton continued. 'While I became a ten-year-old multi-millionaire orphan and was left to rot in a boarding school while my so-called trustees milked the Pallis Group of its most lucrative assets. I was twelve years old by the time Theo won the right to take control of my interests. He took me in. He gave me a home and a more constructive education. When I reached the age of twenty-five, he handed the Pallis Group back to me in a healthier state than it had been before it all happened, then told me to go out there and get on with the job of keeping it that way.'

Zoe's eyelashes fluttered across the glaze of her eyes. 'You love him,' she whispered.

'I love him,' Anton confirmed in a quiet statement of fact. 'He appears hard and tough, but what he really was back then was a lonely man nursing a badly broken heart who needed someone to care about him, just as I needed someone to care what happened to me.'

'So he adopted you.'

'He did not adopt me. He took care of me.'

'And you h-hate my f-father.'

'I don't hate anyone.' He sighed out heavily. 'Unless it's the media mob who threw us both into this situation we now find ourselves in. And even then I can only mildly hate them, because while they have been so busy trying to discover what we are going to do next they have forgotten to check out the past to find out the reason why Leander disappeared in the first place. No, don't faint on me,' he said as she swayed where she sat.

Closing the gap between them at speed, he came to squat down in front of her, picked up her discarded glass of brandy and tried to make her drink some of it, but Zoe shook her head in refusal. Her mind was spinning dizzily with what he'd just said. *Her father's death had thrown them into this situation.*

A situation built on lies, sex and desperately dark secrets. 'We are the past repeating itself,' she whispered. 'And you do want revenge.'

'For crying out loud,' Anton ground out impatiently, 'I do *not* want revenge!'

'So what is it you do want?' Zoe fired back.

Snapping his lips together, he said nothing. Zoe let out a strangled choke of a disbelieving laugh. She could see it all suddenly, and so very clearly. 'You've been pushing for marriage between us almost from the first hour we met. I should have known there was more to it than you wanting to throw the press off our case. What were you intending to do? Were you planning to avenge your mother's humiliation by leaving me standing at the altar while the organ played, *thanks for the memories but I've had what I wanted and made a fool of you, now I'm off*?'

He dared to laugh. Zoe almost lashed out and hit him. Instead she scrambled out from within the circle of his spread thighs and sprang to her feet.

'How, *how* many times do I have to tell you that I don't want Theo's money?' he sighed out impatiently.

'As many times as you've plugged the marriage thing and I still won't believe you—on either count!'

Since he was still holding her glass of brandy, he tossed the liquid to the back of this throat then rid himself of the glass. 'Theo's will has not changed in twenty-three years,' he informed her harshly. 'His son has always been his heir, with any offspring of Leander's next in line in the event of Theo outliving his son! And if you are about to demand how I know all that, then I will tell you,' he ground out, stopping the very words from forming on her trembling lips.

'I hold all of Theo's personal papers because I am the only person he knows he can trust! I will keep faith with that trust no matter what labels others want to hang on me,' he vowed. 'Are you prepared to keep to your promises to me, Zoe?' he said then, facing her off across a two-foot gap that sang with angry challenge. 'Or do you intend to run away from your responsibilities to Theo like your father did?

The room literally rang with his final comment. Zoe stood shivering beneath its angry blast. Everything she had previously believed about her father's exile from his father had just been tipped on its head. Now Anton was slaying her with the full, blunt truth of what her father had done. He'd run away from his responsibilities because he just couldn't face up to them. She didn't blame him for doing it. He'd loved her mother—oh God, how he had proved that—but that was not the issue here. Anton was asking if she was prepared to do for her grandfather what her father had not been prepared to do.

'Theo s-said he didn't want us to get married,' she reminded him.

Reaching out, he grabbed hold of her shoulders. For a few seconds she thought he was going to give her a good shaking but all he did was to hold her in front of him, his eyes and his voice when he spoke intense.

'He was *testing* you. He told you that himself. He was trying to discover if *you* were going to let him down like your father did! He needs to know that his life's legacy will be in safe hands when he dies. So, I am asking you again, are you prepared to be gracious and give your grandfather something good to take with him to his grave?'

Was she prepared to marry the son of the woman her father jilted, to soothe a sick old man's broken heart before he slid quietly out of this life?

Quivering within his grasp, she wished she wasn't

looking into his eyes because when she did that she always—always—lost the will to keep on fighting him.

'Yes,' she heard herself whisper. 'Until my grandfather has—gone,' she extended, because her pride demanded she keep hold of the one concession she had won the last time they had had this kind of fight. 'I will do everything you want me to do until this whole h-horror is over but afterwards I go back to my own life and you will let me go.'

Anton turned as cold as ice, as though she'd thrown a switched that turned off all the passion alight inside him. She did not understand why, and she watched for a sign to give her a hint, but nothing showed in his tough, handsome face. And his continuing silence gnawed on her shivering nerve-ends.

Then he unclasped his fingers. 'Fair enough,' he agreed and turned away.

'Fair enough' sealed their deal in what felt to Zoe like her own fresh blood.

'I'll go and check how Theo is,' he then said flatly, and strode out of the room without looking at her again.

They married a week later right on schedule. Only the venue had changed, moving from the little church on Thalia to a room in her grandfather's house with a magistrate in attendance to hear their vows.

Theo insisted on standing beside Zoe. It was her grandfather who placed her hand into Anton's hand. Only then did he surrender to his wheelchair to watch the rest of the proceedings with a fierce look of satisfaction that was missing on the faces of the other two participants. Once the formalities were over, they drank a glass of champagne each, then Theo caved in and retired to his bed.

He'd looked increasingly frail throughout the short

ceremony, and impulsively Zoe asked if she could see him before she and Anton flew back to Thalia. He was asleep, but she sat with him for a little while, her hand covering one of his, wishing, wishing he'd known her father. Because she was sure he would have been proud of the man he grew to be, even if perhaps he would never have been the kind of son Theo would have preferred him to be. When Anton came in to tell her quietly that it was time for them to leave, she stood up, then she leant down and kissed his cheek before turning and walking quickly away with her head down so that a grimly silent Anton could not see her tears.

Within an hour of arriving back at Anton's house, she felt as if nothing had changed. The simple white wedding-gown she had worn—delivered that morning by special courier—was now hanging in its bag in her dressing room. And, though everyone else had smiles and congratulations for them, she and Anton felt more like strangers to each other than they had done when he had first strode into her Islington home.

It had been like that between them since her visit to see her grandfather. They even slept in their separate bedrooms. Anton was busy, he worked long hours, and though he came home from Athens every evening in time to eat dinner with her, he excused himself and disappeared into his study afterwards and that was the last Zoe would see of him until dinner the next evening.

Seven long days of it, she thought as she stood by the window in her bedroom, having thrown it open to breathe some cooler air coming in from the sea. It wasn't late but she'd retired early. A silvery moon hung just above the tops of the trees. One of the maids—clearly an incurable romantic—had laid out the finest slip of blush-pink silk on her bed, and after taking a shower, she hovered over it for a few moments before giving in to the temptation of slipping the nightdress on.

She caught sight of herself in the mirror, and saw how the silk clung to every contour of her figure, from the slopes of her breasts to her slender ankles.

She looked what she was, a bride dressed for her wedding night. Only this bride had no groom to admire the alluring effect.

Oh, just look at yourself, Zoe told herself crossly, *standing here staring at the moon and pining for your love when—* The soft sound of her bedroom door closing spun her around. As if she'd summoned him up just thinking about him, there he stood, looking tall, dark and breathtakingly real.

'Stargazing, *glikia mou*?' he quizzed as he walked towards her, his voice sounded so deep and so dark it sank through her body like warm honey.

'W-wishing on the moon, more like,' she laughed, trying her best to make it sound light even though her heart began to beat very fast. 'Is—is there something you want?'

'Now that—' he came to a halt in the circle of moonlight '—is a pretty stupid question to ask your husband on our wedding night.'

Her lips parted nervously. 'I thought we had decided to keep this m-marriage strictly business.'

'We did?' He was looking down at her intently but there was no sign that Zoe could see that he'd even heard what she'd said.

And he looked—gorgeous. He had come in here directly from the shower and was wearing a dark cotton robe and nothing else, so her heightened instincts told her. His hair was still damp and as she grabbed at a tense breath she inhaled the tantalising scent of his soap.

She could also feel the tension stretching up through her body like a fine thread of fire. It was all in the eyes—it was always in the eyes for them. He looked down at her and she looked up at him…

'I don't believe I would make such a cold-blooded bargain,' he murmured.

'I thought—' Her voice lurched to a stop as he reached out and touched her, the tips of his fingers gently combing the trailing strands of her hair away from one of her shoulders, before continuing like a caress to curve around her nape, making her draw in a sharp little breath.

'You thought what?' he prompted huskily.

'I…' The words just dried up when he stepped in closer. 'You didn't want me,' she finally managed to squeeze out.

'You chose which bed you wanted to sleep in. I merely respected your wishes.'

Had it really been that simple? Zoe didn't think so. For when had he bothered to respect her wishes before their big showdown in her grandfather's study?

'And now you've chosen not to respect my wishes?' Never one to go down without at least a token fight, she watched the glint of appreciation of that fact light his eyes and he smiled, revealing the edges of his even white teeth.

'Let us agree to say that I knew what you wanted tonight because I want it too.'

And to validate his point he trailed those gentle fingers again, tracing the fine strap to her silk nightdress all the way over a stain-smooth shoulder to the creamy slope of her breast, where the skin was already blooming to the pleasure of his touch.

Lifting up her chin, she looked into his eyes again, his dark, beautiful eyes, then lifted her arms up around his neck. A sigh feathered the aching wall of her throat. 'I've missed you,' she whispered.

It was a shockingly dangerous thing to confess because it left her so exposed and vulnerable. Yet she still reached up to go in search of his mouth. He let her. He let her feather soft kisses across his lips, while he trailed his fingers down the fine silk covering her body, tracing its slender shape.

'No more fighting,' he husked.

'No more fighting,' she agreed, and was rewarded when he took over her soft kisses and turned them into something slow and driving. It felt different, somehow, though she was way too seduced by it to want to work out what why that was. He did not need to draw her against him, because she tilted her head back and arched into him, so his hands only needed to hold her there, warm against him.

They remained like that, kissing in the moonlight coming in through the open window and in no hurry to move things on to the next place. It was just so good to let go of all the restraints they'd been using to hold each other at arm's length all the week. When he did decide it was time to move them he did not pick her up and make a macho charge for his bedroom. He utilised a far more disturbing method, feeding her beneath an arm he rested across her shoulders and walking her there.

She was never going to fight this again—because she knew that she couldn't. Anton Pallis—her lover, her husband—was in her blood and she wanted him to be there. If she'd dared, she would have whispered, 'I love you,' but that was one truth she managed to hold back.

He kissed her again when they stood beside the bed.

Still, slow and sensually alluring, he placed soft-clinging kisses on her face and her throat and eased the straps of her nightdress down her arms until the silky garment slithered sexily down her body to lie in a blush-pink pool at her feet. Drawing back just a little, Zoe lowered her gaze to concentrate on her fingers as they worked to untie the belt on his robe and part it. He did not attempt to help, the vibrations between them were humming as she fed the fabric off his wide shoulders and sent it the same way as her nightdress.

Naked at last—both of them. It felt just so good. When he eased her back against him she breathed out a sigh of pure contentment and pressed her parted lips to his. Her breasts were alive with pleasurable tremors, their distended tips loving the electric rasp against the hair on his chest. He moved against her, using a rhythm older than time, and so beautifully intimate and familiar to her now she even lifted her head up to smile at him.

'You feel glorious,' she told him softly.

'You have just doubled the state of my prowess.' He smiled too.

'I know,' she teased him then without any gap in between; slow and sensual lost out to urgent and hot.

He kept her standing there, though. He did not allow her to sink in a puddle of feelings onto the bed. He aroused her with his kisses and his hands and the proud thrust of his manhood. He brought her to the scintillating edge of her peak then took her over it in one purely masculine move which had him filling her up so he could experience the shimmer of her orgasm, her legs now wrapped around his waist and her fingernails scoring his back.

She loved it that he was trembling. She loved it that she could taste the ragged agony of his breathing inside her mouth and on her tongue. When he finally lowered them down onto the bed to conclude their flaming rise into ecstasy, she cried his name out and he robbed it from her lips with a growl.

The next morning Anton woke her up by dragging her out of the bed.

'What did you do that for!' Zoe snapped at him from the tumbled-haired and sleepy rubble she'd ended up at his feet.

'A surprise,' he announced, and without a single ounce of sympathy for her sleepy grumpiness he bent to lift her up then marched her into the bathroom. 'You have ten minutes to make yourself presentable.'

Ten minutes to the dot, Zoe appeared out of the dressing room wearing shorts and a skimpy camisole-top. 'This had better be a good surprise,' she warned when she found him lounging on the bed waiting for her.

He'd barely let her sleep a wink last night. As far as passionate wedding-nights went, she suspected she'd been treated to the very best. But she was tired now, dull-witted and puffy-eyed, though not so puffy-eyed that she could not appreciate just how sexy he looked in a pair of old grey cut-offs and a white tee-shirt that moulded every impressive muscle—so she didn't have to tax her brain to remember what he looked like without it.

Rolling off the bed, Anton grabbed her hand and trailed her out of the bedroom and down the stairs.

'I haven't even said good morning to Toby!' she complained. 'And I need a cup of tea.'

'Later.' he walked them right past the small dining-room and out into the bright morning sunlight.

At which point Zoe blinked herself so wide awake it was startling.

'Oh my God,' she gasped out.

Standing right in the middle of the garden was the very best surprise he could have come up with. Her eyes took fire with electric-blue delight.

'Where did you get it from? How did you get it here? Oh my *God*!' she repeated with a squeal and took off running barefoot across the springy grass, leaving Anton standing on the terrace watching her through indulgently amused eyes as she danced around the yellow brass telescope glinting in the sun.

He ordered breakfast to be brought out onto the terrace then lounged back on a chair to watch while she tweaked and turned things, chanting out a commentary as to what she was doing which meant absolutely nothing to him. He did not care. His bride was happy. He was seeing the bright, sunny creature he'd always suspected hid behind all the grief and pain of recent weeks. She was glorious, spectacular mix of golden long-limbed beauty, childlike excitement and serious intelligence that quite frankly took his breath away.

By the time night fell on Thalia he was beginning to wonder if he'd made a tactical mistake. He'd taken second place to a damn telescope. For a man who had never been second to anything or anyone in his adult life, the blow to his ego was tough to take. In the end he went off to his study to catch up on some work while Zoe spent the whole day pouring over the heavy manuals and checking the internet for stargazing stuff that passed right over his head.

Even Toby barely got a look in. 'You and I have been abandoned,' Anton informed the boy who stayed awake longer now and listened with a fierce concentration when someone talked to him. 'We have been sidelined by a tube of brass with a fancy glass lens.'

Diamonds might have been a better choice, he mused

ruefully. Then discarded the idea of any diamond exciting Zoe like his wedding gift had done.

By nightfall Zoe was ready to remember Anton's presence, and was beginning to feel guilty for the way she'd forgotten about him all day. She hadn't even got round to saying thank you for giving her such a fabulous surprise.

For once all the drilling she'd suffered from Anthea came in useful; she decided to set right that omission. She had a roomful of rattan furniture hauled out onto the grass while Anton stayed shut away in his study. Then she arranged with Anthea for them to eat dinner out there by soft, romantic candlelight. She changed into the sexiest dress she could find on her rail of clothes—a skimpy, slinky blood-red silk thing which clung to her figure much like last night's nightdress had done, only the dress finished high up her long slender thighs.

His eyes turned polished black when he saw her. Her hair shone as brightly as the lustrous smile on her lips. She took his hand, trailed him outside and fed him his favourite food—according to Anthea—and teased him terribly by assuring him he was going to love the surprises she had in store for him later. She was going to let him see what she saw when she looked through her lovely, wonderful new telescope.

And she did. She made him look through the lens at the coordinates she'd carefully set up. She gave him a lecture on that far-distant spot in the heavens as seen from his garden, and refused to notice that he was bored out of his handsome, dark head. When eventually she let him pop the cork on the champagne bottle, he looked so relieved she almost laughed.

'Now,' she said, pushing him down onto the rattan sofa. 'Time for your wedding gift from me.'

Curiously, Anton watched her step back to the table and

put down her glass. Even more curiously, he watched as she fed her hands up beneath her dress, wriggled out of a pair of flimsy red-lace panties and dropped them on the grass.

No longer needing to hide his boredom, he was suddenly riveted to what was about to take place. For he knew what was coming. He'd been seduced too many times not to recognise the build-up. However, this was different. This was his bride—his reluctant bride—and the heat already dancing around his loins caught fire as she walked over to him then slowly straddled his lap.

'You're supposed to be impressed,' Zoe told him. 'It's the first time I've tried a full-on seduction.'

'I am impressed,' he assured her. 'But we are outside, *agape mou*, where anyone can see us.'

'Oh, you prude,' she pouted in disappointment and lifted his glass to her lips.

Her eyes were twinkling at him brighter than the star-light sky he'd just been forced to admire. 'You have this problem covered, don't you?' he murmured, raising a sleek black-satin eyebrow.

'I am by nature a very organised kind of person,' Zoe confirmed, deadpan.

Deadpan, because she was moving ever so slightly against him, so she knew exactly what was happening to him. 'Do you want a sip?' She offered the glass back to him. He took it and tossed it away into the night. Zoe watched the glass fly through the air until it landed on the grass. 'Well, that was a very imaginative way of answering me,' she murmured.

'And you, wife, are a dreadful tease,' he threw back.

She was not just a tease, she was a seductive tease. Without removing her eyes from his, she fed her hands down and began tugging his shirt free from his trousers.

'You want me naked,' he surmised.

'Yes please.' She nodded.

That he was already heeling his shoes off said he was ahead of her anyway. She unbuttoned his shirt and spread it wide then bent to taste the salty warmth of his skin. On a muttered curse, Anton dragged the shirt off altogether then wrapped his bare arms around her and demanded she lift her head. The first kiss was everything Zoe wanted. It spun them down into a darkened world of sultry heat and sensual caresses. Only when she needed to tell him that she wanted him inside her did she lift her hands up to frame his face.

'Thank you,' she whispered. 'For my surprise.'

Then she raised up her hips and lowered them slowly, taking him deep, deep inside. The way he closed his eyes and breathed unsteadily, *'Thee mou,'* made her feel like the happiest new bride on this earth.

CHAPTER TWELVE

ZOE forgot to keep reminding herself that this was only temporary. That it was a straight business-deal with a lot of hot sex thrown in. She was happy. After weeks of feeling so unhappy it was like dragging a heavy weight around with her, she allowed herself to embrace her new life in Greece with Anton by pushing to the back of her head any small pangs of doubt that occasionally crept in.

Then, four weeks later, reality arrived with a painful thump. Her grandfather passed away quietly in his sleep. A lawyer came out from Athens to read them his last will and testament. Other than for the expected provisions made for those people Theo had cared about, and had cared about him, the bulk of the estate went to Zoe and Toby. Anton retaining control of all business interests until such time as if and when they divorced, at which point his granddaughter would be free to make her own arrangements. There was very little either she or Anton could say. It was exactly how Anton had always said it would be, and she'd stopped disbelieving him so long ago it was a distant memory.

She left him to deal with the lawyer while she made herself scarce, spending the next few hours with her brother, sending Melissa away so she could sink herself into the comforting routine of caring for the baby by herself.

When Anton eventually came looking for her it was

late, way beyond the time they would normally sit down for dinner. He found her lying on one of the loungers in the garden, silently mapping stars while she tried to keep her thoughts at bay.

For this was it, the moment she had been putting off in some vague hope it would never happen. But it had happened and now she had to think about hers and Toby's future away from this place. Away from Anton and their marriage of convenience, which had never felt to her like a business agreement even though that was exactly what it was.

She'd been offered a job working at the observatory in Athens. The offer had come out of the blue only a few days ago, via her professor in Manchester. It was almost too good to be true, she mused, whispering a sigh up into the dark sky. She could pay off her student loans and not miss the cash, and she and Toby could move into her grandfather's house in Glyfada. After all, she had all the money in the world now to ease the path for any decision she wanted to make. Melissa could come with them. She could hire her own staff.

Or she could continue to bury her head in the sand and do absolutely nothing. And why was she considering that as an option? Because she did not want to leave here, this island, this house…

'Not eating tonight?' Hearing the even-pitched voice—belonging to the big reason why she didn't want to leave here—Zoe turned her head to watch as Anton stretched out beside her on the other lounger. It was really quite funny the way they'd formed their own private living area out here on the lawn over the last few weeks.

Only Zoe wasn't laughing. In fact she felt so unhappy she wanted to cry. She looked back at the night sky again and watched it blur out of focus.

'Theo asked me only the day before he died if I still hated him,' she confided.

Threading his long fingers with hers, he asked, 'What did you say?'

'I told him the truth. I told him that at first I wanted to hate him but when I looked at him I saw my own father, so how could I hate the man who gave me the love of the most wonderful father I could have had?'

'You made your peace with him, *agape mou*,' Anton said gently. 'That is a good thing.'

Pressing her trembling lips together, Zoe nodded her head. 'I—liked him.'

'For all his irascible manner, Theo kind of grows on you,' Anton said with a smile. Then he stopped smiling. 'However, he has become yet another person you cared about who has passed out of your life.'

Another person she cared for she'd lost… That was three people already this year, and now she was having to come to terms with the knowledge that she was about to lose another one.

On impulse she lifted their clasped hands and pressed kisses on his fingers. 'I've been offered a job,' she whispered tragically.

She felt his fingers tighten on her fingers before he untangled them, and wished she could learn to hang on to secrets as well as he did.

'A good one?' he asked after a tense moment.

'Yes,' she confirmed, then went on to explain. 'It feels like those heavens up there have been pulling strings for me down here. If I take the job it will mean I can finish my post-grad course while I work—get some normality back in my life. You too,' she added carefully, aware that she was opening the can of worms she had wanted to keep sealed up so tight no one would be able to prise off the lid.

'My life is fine the way that it is,' Anton responded smoothly. 'We can both commute,' he decided then. 'I do it every day as it is.'

'You know that wasn't what I meant.' Sitting up, she wrapped her arms around her bent knees. He wasn't so slow on the uptake that he hadn't already worked out where she was going with this. 'We had an—arrangement,' she spelled it out. 'Now it's time for us to—bring it an end.'

For a minute his silence was agony. For a minute she even questioned whether or not he had heard what she'd said. She wanted to look at him, but she couldn't bring herself to look, and the tears were rolling freely down her cheeks.

He sat up too, only he *got* up, rising to his full height and shoving his hands into his trouser pockets. 'Don't do this, Zoe,' he growled out.

'Don't do what—talk about the thing we have both been hiding away from here? Theo is *gone*.' Feeling the need to bite down on something to stop the sobs from forming in her throat, she bit down hard on one of her knees.

'And if you are trying to tell me that you want out of this marriage because of Theo's death, then try telling me so with a bit more enthusiasm than that stupid comment muffled by the thickness of your tears!'

So, she was crying… Zoe used the back of her hand to wipe her damp cheeks. 'I don't see why you're so angry. This has always only been only a temporary s-situation.'

'It is not a *situation*, it is a *marriage*!' He launched down at her. 'I *married* you, I did not *buy* you in some cut-throat *arrangement* I made with Theo or you or the damn devil himself. I married you. I wanted you to be my *wife*.' He tossed the words down at her like Zeus throwing thunder-bolts. 'How many times did I offer to marry you before we eventually did it?'

'*Offer!* I beg your pardon?' Zoe scrambled to her feet. 'You never *offered* to do anything!' she flashed back at him. 'You *told* me what I had to do because you always think that you know best!'

'I do always know best,' he countered savagely. 'Why else are we having this ridiculous argument? Because you started it.' He snapped out the answer to his own question. 'Because you can be such a flimsy-brained idiot when—'

'How dare you call me flimsy-brained?' Zoe gasped.

He could because he was angry. He could because he had truly believed that she had more damn sense by now than to still think of their marriage as temporary.

'You are so rude sometimes.'

She stiffened up like a long, slender soldier with tangled golden hair wearing skimpy shorts and a top that did absolutely nothing to hide the lush curves beneath it. Anton looked her over with a derisive flick of a gaze.

'Don't come the lofty English lady with me,' he retorted. 'You are as Greek as I am underneath all of that haughty dignity. You are as stubborn as I am and just as determined to get your own way as I am. You are also a hell of a lot better at making me suffer for my sins than I've made you suffer.'

Opening her eyes very wide, Zoe stared at him. 'I have never made you suffer!'

'What the hell are you doing to me now?' He flung angry arms out, then turned his back on her. 'I love you,' he raked out into the darkened garden. 'And all you can say to me is you want out.'

Shocked into uttering a choked gasp, she whispered, 'Oh, that's so unfair. Love is not what we've been about and you know it.'

His derisive laugh sprang into the night. 'Not for you, no.'

'Not for you either!' Zoe yelled at the top of her agitated voice. 'So if—if you want me and Toby to stay with you out of some n-need to fulfil your promise to Theo, then just s-say so—but don't you *dare* call it love!'

Her shrill voice pitched into a startled yelp when he spun on her and grabbed hold of her by her shoulders. She was trying to wipe a fresh set of tears from her cheeks when he gave her a rough kind of shake.

'Look at me,' he bit out, because she was looking at the ground between them. When she refused to lift her head up he gave her another small shake. 'Look at me, Zoe,' he repeated deeply.

Reluctant and defiant about it, Zoe lifted her eyes up to his.

'Now.' He cinched in a short breath. 'Tell me what you see.'

She knew exactly what she saw but there was no way she was going to tell him what it was. She went to pull away from him but his fingers only tightened their grip. 'You are not moving from this spot until you look at me and tell me what you see!'

'All right!' She broke down on a sob of helplessness. 'I see the man I've fallen in love with.' There, she'd said it, but unlike him she meant every wretched, heartbreaking word. 'Are you h-happy now?'

Seemingly no, Anton was not happy because, when she tried to break free of him so she could run away to some deep dark corner somewhere and hide in agony, he held her fast with those strong fingers.

'No,' he denied her her wish. 'What you see when you look at me, *agape mou*, is the man who loves you. The same way it is when I look at you and see the women who loves *me*. Think about it,' he stressed. 'From the moment our eyes met in your London kitchen—every time since then that we do this we see it and know what it is. You are already melting for me, you know you are. Why can't you see that it has always been the same for me?'

Did she see it? Did she dare to see it? It was a wildly crazy thought, but had she been so busy hiding from what she was feeling for him that she'd blinded herself to what he was feeling of her?

She was already melting into his deep, dark burning eyes.

'Say something,' he demanded when she just stood and stared at him—stared *into* him—ripped him open and scooped him out. And if she didn't speak in the next second he was going to…

'Oh Anton.' In a convulsive lurch she reached up and wound her arms around his neck. 'I've been so *miserable* thinking I was going to have to leave you!'

'Then you should have known better.' He hauled her closer. 'When,' he demanded, 'Have I ever let you leave me?'

Never, thought Zoe. Not once, even when he'd kidnapped her and scared her into hysterics and felt really bad about it afterwards. Then there was the night he had first made love to her, and he'd felt really guilty about doing that—but he had not given her the option of leaving. Not this man who always believed he was in the right.

'I need you to kiss me,' she whispered.

He did not need telling twice. On a lusty growl, he lowered his dark head and crushed her lips with his. It was not the most passionate kiss they had shared—too many other emotions cluttering it up. Still, she had to cling to his neck when he let her up for air again, and she revelled in the accelerated beat of his heart.

Zoe lifted her darkened eyes back to his. 'I love you so much, it's scary,' she confided. *'S'agapo,'* she whispered, because it felt so right to repeat it in Greek. 'Now you say it in case I misheard you.'

So he did. He said it in Greek, he said it in English; he even said it in Russian and a dozen other languages as he walked them across the garden and into the house.

'Are you two ready for dinner now?' Anthea paused on her way to the small dining-room.

'Later,' said Anton, his arm around Zoe's shoulders as they started up the stairs.

Anthea just sighed and returned to her kitchen, though there was a smile on her lips, because she did not need to study the stars to know where the two of them were off to now. Anton closed the bedroom door behind them. The house eventually settled into its late-night hush.

'If I live to be a hundred I will never get enough of you,' he groaned after the kind of loving that left them both in a state of boneless release.

With her cheek resting against his chest, Zoe smiled sleepily. 'I'll remind you of that when the day comes.'

'OK,' he yawned. 'That sounds like a good deal to me.'

It was a silly conversation but Zoe liked it. She wriggled closer to him and draped her leg over both of his. 'Love you,' she mumbled as her eyes grew heavy.

'Love you too, *glikia mou*,' he returned—but Zoe was already asleep.

* * * * *

Coming Next Month

from **Harlequin Presents® EXTRA.** Available October 11, 2011.

#169 IN WANT OF A WIFE?
Cathy Williams
The Powerful and the Pure

#170 THE RETURN OF THE STRANGER
Kate Walker
The Powerful and the Pure

#171 THE S BEFORE EX
Mira Lyn Kelly
Tabloid Scandals

#172 SEX, GOSSIP AND ROCK & ROLL
Nicola Marsh
Tabloid Scandals

Coming Next Month

from **Harlequin Presents®.** Available October 25, 2011.

#3023 THE MOST COVETED PRIZE
Penny Jordan
Russian Rivals

#3024 THE MAN WITH THE MONEY
Lynn Raye Harris
The Notorious Wolfes

#3025 JEWEL IN HIS CROWN
Lynne Graham

#3026 THE ICE PRINCE
Sandra Marton
The Orsini Brides

#3027 THE PRICE OF SCANDAL
Kim Lawrence

#3028 A ROYAL ENGAGEMENT
Trish Morey and Caitlin Crews

Harlequin® Special Edition® is thrilled to present a new installment in USA TODAY *bestselling author RaeAnne Thayne's reader-favorite miniseries,* THE COWBOYS OF COLD CREEK.

Join the excitement as we meet the Bowmans—four siblings who lost their parents but keep family ties alive in Pine Gulch. First up is Trace. Only two things get under this rugged lawman's skin: beautiful women and secrets. And in Rebecca Parsons, he finds both!

Read on for a sneak peek of CHRISTMAS IN COLD CREEK. Available November 2011 from Harlequin® Special Edition®.

On impulse, he unfolded himself from the bar stool. "Need a hand?"

"Thank you! I…" She lifted her gaze from the floor to his jeans and then raised her eyes. When she identified him her hazel eyes turned from grateful to unfriendly and cold, as if he'd somehow thrown the broken glasses at her head.

He also thought he saw a glimmer of panic in those interesting depths, which instantly stirred his curiosity like cream swirling through coffee.

"I've got it, Officer. Thank you." Her voice was several degrees colder than the whirl of sleet outside the windows.

Despite her protests, he knelt down beside her and began to pick up shards of broken glass. "No problem. Those trays can be slippery."

This close, he picked up the scent of her, something fresh and flowery that made him think of a mountain meadow on a July afternoon. She had a soft, lush mouth and for one brief, insane moment, he wanted to push aside that stray lock of hair slipping from her ponytail and taste her. Apparently he needed to spend a lot less time working and a great deal *more* time recreating with the opposite sex if he could have sudden random fantasies about a woman he wasn't even inclined to like, pretty or not.

"I'm Trace Bowman. You must be new in town."

She didn't answer immediately and he could almost see the wheels turning in her head. Why the hesitancy? And why that little hint of unease he could see clouding the edge of her gaze? His presence was obviously making her uncomfortable and Trace couldn't help wondering why.

"Yes. We've been here a few weeks."

"Well, I'm just up the road about four lots, in the white house with the cedar shake roof, if you or your daughter need anything." He smiled at her as he picked up the last shard of glass and set it on her tray.

Definitely a story there, he thought as she hurried away. He just might need to dig a little into her background to find out why someone with fine clothes and nice jewelry, and who so obviously didn't have experience as a waitress, would be here slinging hash at The Gulch. Was she running away from someone? A bad marriage?

So...Rebecca Parsons. Not Becky. An intriguing woman. It had been a long time since one of those had crossed his path here in Pine Gulch.

Trace won't rest until he finds out Rebecca's secret, but will he still have that same attraction to her once he does?
Find out in CHRISTMAS IN COLD CREEK.
Available November 2011 from Harlequin® Special Edition®.

HSEEXP1111